Remind Me Why I'm Here

Remind Me Why I'm Here

© Kat Colmer, 2020

Published by Rhiza Edge, 2020
An imprint of Rhiza Press
PO Box 1519,
Capalaba QLD 4159
Australia
www.rhizaedge.com.au

Cover design by Rhiza Press through Book Whispers
Layout by Rhiza Press

Print ISBN: 978-1-925563-92-4

A catalogue record for this
book is available from the
National Library of Australia

Remind Me Why I'm Here

Kat Colmer

rhiza edge

For Nathalia,
who loved and believed
in this story from the start.

Chapter One

The absence of water made Maya nervous.

Barangaroo, with its famous harbour-side views, should have been no more than half an hour from the airport. So where were the white Opera House sails? The Sydney Harbour Bridge? All that greeted her out the car window was the late afternoon sun casting shadows across an ever increasing number of parched grass paddocks.

Something wasn't right.

She tapped the map app on her cell and her eyes widened—the blue dot marking the car's location was moving *away* from the coastline. Away from Sydney's inner city.

Away from her destination suburb of Barangaroo.

'Um, excuse me.' Maya poked her head between the car's front seats. 'Aren't we meant to have arrived already?'

The fifty-something orange-haired woman—Brenda, according to the driver information on the dash—lifted her smiling gaze to the rearview mirror. 'No, love. We've got a ways to go yet.'

Maya's stomach dropped. Maybe she'd misread the GPS times and directions. Back in Chicago, everyone had warned her the distances were much greater Down Under than people thought.

'We're heading to Barangaroo, right?' No harm in asking, just to be on the safe side.

There was an orange-haired nod.

Maya slumped in her seat with relief. Maybe the driver was taking the scenic route so she could clock more miles on the metre? *Unlikely.* This lady seemed honest down to her Fanta-coloured roots.

'Barangaroo Creek, Miss,' the driver added. 'Excellent sheep farming down this way.'

Maya jolted upright. 'I'm sorry, did you say *sheep* farming?'

'Indeed. We're heading into some of the best Merino sheep country in the whole land.'

Sheep country? Maya's stomach hit the fake leather of the car's back seat about the same time her jaw smacked her chest.

'I think there's been a mistake. I'm meant to go to *Barangaroo.*' She thrust her head between the front seats again. 'You know, the harbour-side suburb in the city? I think you've picked up the wrong person.'

That had to be it. It was a mix-up. A massive mix-up. They should turn around. Some other poor girl named Mia or Meeha was probably scratching her head, watching boats float by on Sydney Harbour and wondering where all the sheep had gone.

The driver's puzzled gaze met Maya's in the rearview mirror. 'You're Maya Sorenson from Chicago, Illinois?'

Maya forced herself to nod, sending an errant strand of hair into her eyes.

'Then there's no mistake.' The driver plucked a sheet of paper from the passenger seat and handed it to her. 'Says here I'm to take you to Barangaroo Creek, Miss, not the city.'

Maya wound the annoying bit of hair around her finger and wedged it behind her ear as she scanned the page.

Passenger name: Maya Sorensen.

Destination: Barangaroo Creek.

No. No no no. This *had* to be a mistake. Animals and her … Not a good idea.

She opened the map app on her phone again and typed

Barangaroo Creek into the search box. The blue dot took off and landed somewhere about three and a half hours south west of Sydney.

Maya's lungs stopped functioning for a solid five seconds, then filled with a desperate breath and a double dose of dread. A *sheep farm*? Of all the places on earth, a sheep farm? This wasn't good. Total recipe for disaster. Her freshman year field trip to a dairy farm, she'd ended up hospitalised with concussion. Apparently, you *can* tug a cow's teat the wrong way.

This had to be a mistake. But whose?

Unease prickled at her nape. She hadn't paid much attention to the details of the trip. For her, it was all about the *List*. Maya glanced out at the thirsty paddocks whizzing past the window and winced. Could she really have messed up this badly?

With a shaky hand, she flicked to her parents' numbers in her favourites list, then paused. It had been late when she'd spoken to them after landing an hour ago. Now, four in the afternoon in Sydney made it midnight the previous night in Chicago. Dad had to be at the workshop in five hours. She'd hate to wake him. Mum, on the other hand, might still be up, eyeball deep in case notes or some such. The fortress of cases she'd steadily built around herself these past twelve months was a protection Maya understood.

Her finger hovered over her mum's number but pressed the message icon instead. She didn't want anything in her voice giving away this monumental stuff-up. Mum and Dad were worried enough about her current state of mind.

Hey Mom, you still up?

Three tell-tale little dots danced across her screen in answer to the question.

Yes. Find the car we organised ok?

In it now and on our way. Just wondering about something—

How to phrase this without giving herself away—

How do I do the Bridge Climb and Opera House if I'm staying on a sheep farm?

The little dots bounced along with Maya's jittery leg. She stared at the screen, willing phrases like 'What are you talking about?' or 'What sheep farm?' to appear and quash her growing dread.

A weekend trip into Sydney is part of the farm stay package. Did you miss that bit in the information booklet?

Maya blinked, her mother's reply on the screen suddenly hazy. Even so, the words 'farm stay package' jumped at her through the sudden fog, clawing at her throat, making it difficult to breathe. *Sheep farm.* She whimpered. *I'm spending the next six weeks on a SHEEP FARM!*

How had she been so oblivious as to miss this small—read ENORMOUS—detail?

Maya? Everything ok?

Maya stared at her mother's text. Her silent scream at the horror of her situation must have been loud enough for her mother to hear all the way back in Chicago.

Her fingers flew over the keypad. *No, Mom! Everything is not ok!* Breath tight and quick, she stared at the words; at their truth so much deeper than Barangaroo Creek and sheep and unwanted farm stays. She sucked in an unsteady breath. There was only one thing to do. She hit the backspace until the words were gone and typed new ones.

Must have skimmed that part of the information booklet.

Maya cringed. She'd skimmed her way through most of the planning of the trip like she'd skimmed her way through most of twelfth grade this year. Sure, she'd caught words like 'Sydney' and 'Barangaroo', and when she found the strength to push aside the fog that had swallowed her this past year, she'd skimmed her way through some internet research, which promised her sparkling blue water, harbour-side cafes, and a funky looking Opera House. Except, she wasn't headed for Sydney's Barangaroo. No, she was barrelling towards sheep-filled Barangaroo *Creek!* The enormity of her stuff-up started to set in. Worse yet, if her parents realised her head was still so screwed-up that she had no clue where she was meant to be spending the next month and a half, they'd haul her back home on the next flight.

That, she couldn't have. She reached for the leather band on her left wrist and thumbed its comforting texture.

I'll have another read of it tonight, she typed and meant it.

Sheep or no sheep, she couldn't leave. Not without completing the *List*.

Call when you've settled in.

Maya sent a thumbs up in reply. She noticed her fingernails were short, clipped, clean. No more greasy ghosts under them to remind her that her brother's obsession had once been her favourite pastime, too. She turned the leather strap on her wrist, round and round and round, like a newly replaced fan belt. She missed it, the smell of cold metal and worn car parts; the clang of tools as Michael patiently showed her what went where and which parts did what. But not as much as she missed him.

Maya met Brenda's confused gaze in the mirror. 'You're right. I'm heading to Barangaroo Creek.' She smiled in apology and skimmed—*No! No more skimming*—read the paperwork closely for her host sister's name. *Ruth.* A sensible name. Hopefully Ruth wouldn't mind helping her tick off the items on her *List*. Even if she didn't, Maya would complete all seven of them. There was no question of that. She had to. It was the only way she knew how to make amends.

Chapter Two

'What do you mean Ruth won't be here for the next six weeks?' Gus generally avoided using a sharp tone with his parents, especially his mother, but he'd just spent the day watering and feeding stock in temperatures high enough to deep fry battered fish, so he wasn't in the mood for jokes. Especially not bad ones. All he wanted was a cold shower and to finish packing.

His mother looked up from the tomato she was chopping. Her pinched expression had him worried. 'Aunt Cecily has been prescribed complete bed rest until the baby comes. She can't run around after the twins. She needs help. It was either Ruth or you, and Ruth jumped at the chance. She was adamant you'd prefer to spend the next six weeks in the company of someone your own age rather than two overenthusiastic three-year-olds.'

Gus huffed. Yeah, he'd prefer to spend the next six weeks in the company of people his own age. In *Sydney*. On the trip he had all booked and planned.

Not with some girl from the States he didn't even know.

Under other circumstances, he'd have been happy to play host to yet another homestay guest. It made Mum happy, sharing a slice of 'Aussie farm life' with people from all corners of the world. The Italian guy last year had been a hoot. But this year—and this girl—

was Ruth's responsibility. They'd all agreed.

'I've been looking forward to this holiday for months.' Gus tried to keep his voice level, but his frustration came through in every clipped word. 'Everything's already paid for.'

'If that's what you're worried about, I'll repay the damn money.' His father's baritone rumble came from the open side door. A slap of his Akubra against his thigh sent dust clouding around his tall frame. 'Family is more important than flailing about on some surfboard with your friends,' he said, sitting down at the kitchen table.

His father seemed to have forgotten that Gus was also part of this family and this trip was important to *him*.

'This girl's what … seventeen?'

'Eighteen,' his mother said.

Even better. 'Eighteen, so legally an adult.' Gus stepped closer to the kitchen table. 'She'll be fine without a babysitter for a few weeks and the two of you'll be around, so—'

'No.' His father didn't even bother looking up from the magazine he was flicking through. 'With the weather the way it is and the herd needing handfeeding, your mother and I will be busy enough. You'll stay here and take Ruth's place as host for the American girl.'

And that was that. No 'could you'. No 'please'. No thought to how Gus might feel about having to miss out on this last bit of freedom before he started at the agricultural college, something he didn't want to do in the first place.

Gus opened his mouth to argue but snapped it shut at the familiar hard line of his father's lips. There was no point arguing. There never had been. Not when it came to trivial decisions like having ice cream instead of custard with their Sunday apple pie, or life-altering ones like Gus having to take over the farm instead of Pat. Gus's father thought the surfing holiday was a waste of time, so that certainly wasn't going to sway his opinion. When Richard Thomas Robertson spoke, his words may as well have been etched in stone, because what he said was law. At least around here.

Usually Gus grit his teeth and got over it quickly, but this time … this time was different. He didn't much care about the ice cream on the stupid pie, and guilt had led him to accept that he had to step into Pat's shoes, but this Sydney trip was meant to have been his last *hoorah*. His one chance to carve his own path, even if just for a few weeks. His tiny taste of what could have been if Pat hadn't …

Pat.

'Can't Pat do it?' Entertaining an exchange student wasn't exactly difficult … or dangerous.

His father scoffed. 'Don't talk nonsense. The idea is to show the girl around the place, give her a real taste of farm life. Your brother can't do that.'

Movement drew Gus's gaze to the kitchen doorway. He didn't know how long Pat had been there, but the thin line of his older brother's mouth told him he'd heard enough.

Gus bit down on his sudden flare of anger, for both himself and his brother. Their father calmly leafed through a farm machinery catalogue. With his face lined and leathered by years in the unforgiving sun, and hands cut and calloused, he personified life on the land.

His father loved it like Pat always had. The break-of-dawn starts, the relentless summer heat, the freezing winter mornings, the predictable cycle of farm life and death. Gus, on the other hand, often wondered if he'd been swapped at birth. He didn't hate the land, but he didn't crave it like they did.

Not like he craved … He shook his head, throwing off the thought before it fully formed.

This absence of attachment for the land weighed heavily on Gus. The Sydney trip was a betrayal, and if his father ever found out how Gus was planning to spend the next six weeks, this sheep farmer's son would be disowned.

'Go wash up,' his mother told him from the stove where she stirred pasta sauce. 'The girl should be here in time for dinner.'

He let go of the kitchen chair he'd been gripping way too tightly and ran a hand through his dust and sweat caked hair. He was sore from scalp to sole and would kill for a long soak in a cool bath. And if he stayed in the kitchen much longer, he'd only end up lashing out at his father—an exercise that never ended well.

He passed his brother, catching his eye in a look of shared frustration, and was halfway down the hallway when the crunch of tyres outside slowed his steps.

'No time to wash up now,' his father called from the kitchen. 'She's here.'

Great. Gus took a resigned breath and turned back around to welcome his unwanted visitor.

And kiss goodbye any chance he'd had of spending the next six weeks doing what he really loved.

Chapter Three

The heat hit Maya first. Followed closely by the dry, earthy smell. And then the flies. So many flies! Screwing up her nose, Maya stepped out onto the dusty, packed dirt of the driveway and looked around. All that met her was empty yellow-brown grass-filled paddock, next to empty yellow-brown grass-filled paddock, next to empty yellow-brown grass-filled—*Wait,* did that one have alpacas in it? She liked alpacas about as much as she liked cows. Or sheep. Or anything with more than two legs, really.

'Here you go.' The driver plonked Maya's suitcase at her feet. 'You'll be fine, Miss.' The Fanta-haired woman offered her a reassuring smile. Was her worry that obvious? Maya caught her own reflection in the car's window and—yep, her face might as well have had the words *Get me out of this backwater town now!* written on it.

Maya swung her backpack over her shoulder and turned toward the house. Make that a homestead. Hand shielding her face from the setting sun's glare, Maya took in the single-storey structure. What it lacked in height it made up for in impressive width; the sandstone frontage seemed to stretch forever. A corrugated iron roof atop a wooden veranda skirted the entire length of the front and wrapped around the sides. A set of stairs, five rungs tall, ran the span of the deck, split only by a small ramp to the right.

The bang of a flyscreen cut through the incessant drone of what sounded like a gazillion crickets rubbing at a mega case of athlete's foot. Out stepped a sturdy woman wearing a pale pink sleeveless cotton shirt and a pair of dark blue shorts. Her smile was so wide its corners stabbed Maya in the gut with guilt for having thought words like *backwater town.*

'Welcome.' The smile grew wider as the woman approached. 'We've been expecting you. I'm Jenny Robertson. You can call me Jen.' She held out a tanned, work-roughened hand for a no-nonsense handshake. Jen nodded at the driver over Maya's shoulder and the car's engine spat to life. Moments later, the uber wound its way up the long red dirt driveway to the main road. Maya swallowed. *No way out of this now.*

Jen took hold of Maya's suitcase. 'You're just in time for dinner, but I imagine you'll want to clean up, maybe have a rest first?'

'That'd be nice, thank you.' Maya forced a smile and followed Jen. Some time alone to let this new version of her trip sink in was exactly what she needed.

Another bang of the flyscreen brought Maya's eyes to the front door again. Her feet slowed at the sight: blue cotton shirt sleeves rolled up, thumbs hooked into the pockets of dirt-smeared jeans. A guy about her age leaned against one of the veranda posts and watched her from beneath the rim of a tattered cowboy hat. The only thing about him that said *welcome* was the small brown-and-white dog at his feet, tail wagging furiously. Maya sighed. *This trip just keeps getting better and better.*

'My youngest son, Angus.' Jen's voice propelled Maya's feet back into normal motion. 'Don't just stand there, Gus. Introduce yourself and give us a hand with the luggage.'

Maya only managed a few steps before Gus's long strides had him standing in front of her. Up close, she could see his hair was a couple of shades lighter than her own almost-black not-quite curls. His eyes were a closer match—a deep earth brown. Even with the frown creasing his

11

tanned features, Maya had to admit the guy was cute.

'Hi, I'm Gus.' The smile he offered Maya as he took her luggage didn't make it to his eyes. *What was up with that?*

At least the dog wasn't the yappy, jumpy type and left her alone after it sniffed at her feet.

And hopefully her host sister had a better attitude than Farmer Boy. They climbed the front steps to the house and Maya scanned the veranda for a female teenage face.

Jen must have seen her looking around. 'Now, you might be expecting to meet our daughter, Ruth. Unfortunately, she's had to leave to help out with an urgent … family matter.' Jen's voice dropped on the last two words and took Maya's sinking expectations for the rest of the day with it.

'I'm sorry to hear that. I can wait till tomorrow to meet her.'

'That won't be possible.' Jen frowned in apology. 'She'll be gone for the rest of the summer.'

Maya's mouth dried up. Gone for the *rest* of the summer?

'No need to worry,' Jen said, opening the flyscreen door. 'Gus here will look after you instead.'

Perfect.

Maya's gaze snapped to meet Gus's across the wide entryway they'd stepped into. The smile he gave her was brief and tight and full of forced obligation. No prizes for guessing how he felt about this arrangement.

'Why don't you show Maya to her room while I go check on dinner,' Jen said, disappearing through what Maya assumed to be the kitchen door.

'This way.' Gus led the way down a long hallway. With Jen gone, Maya had no choice but to follow. They walked past several closed doors on the left, as well as a living area to the right, until they arrived at an open door towards the end of the hallway.

The room wasn't fancy. At one end of it stood a wood-framed double bed and a beat-up old wardrobe; at the other, a writing desk sat beside a set of glass doors leading out onto the veranda. A quilt lay across the bed, its intricate pattern of greens and burgundies adding a splash of colour to the space. That, and the sunburnt evening light filtering through the window, gave the space an inviting enough feel.

Gus heaved Maya's suitcase onto the bed and turned to face her. 'Bathroom's across the hall. Towels and other linen are in the cupboard halfway down the hallway.' He waved out the door then to the right like some misguided flight attendant pointing out emergency exits. 'If you need to freshen up or whatever, I'd appreciate it if you did it now. I've been in the paddocks all day and I'd really like to shower before dinner. You know, shared bathroom and all.' Face plastered with another of his tight-lipped smiles, he crossed his arms and waited for her response.

What was the *deal* with this dude? Was he always this uptight?

The little research she'd done said Aussies were a friendly and laid-back bunch. Okay, maybe that was stereotyping, but what was this guy's problem? Then again, all the dust and heat and sheep dung would beat the laid-back out of her too.

Maya zipped open her suitcase and pulled out her toiletries bag. 'Give me five and the bathroom is all yours.' Her tone was as sweet as Farmer Boy's was uptight.

He grunted. She fought the urge to pull his stupid cowboy hat down over his eyes as she slid past him out the door.

Right now, the chance to splash some cold water on her face was more important than working out what had crawled up the Down Under cowboy's nose and short-circuited the part of his brain in charge of personality. If the guy didn't loosen up soon it was going to be a long six weeks for both of them.

In the bathroom, Maya caught her reflection and cringed. Somehow she managed to look both flushed and sullen at the same time. The long flight, the city-farm mix-up, the heat, the sheep— even though she hadn't actually yet *seen* any sheep … She was tired and frustrated, and now she had to put up with Gus, who clearly wished she'd landed in someone else's sheep paddock.

She turned on the tap, stuck her hands under the faucet and groaned; the water ran lukewarm. *That'd be right.* She just couldn't catch a break today.

Maya sighed and gave her face a wash with the tepid water, then quickly brushed her teeth. The water tasted of … nothing. No chlorine or fluoride or whatever else was usually in drinking water. Was that even safe? Another thing to worry about out here. She mentally made a note to Google *outback water* later.

She so needed to unload with Emmy.

Back in her bedroom, there was no sight of Gus. *Thank God.* She fished her cell out of her backpack and frowned. She'd bought an Australian SIM card back at the airport, but her cell showed only one tiny bar of reception and zero data coverage. Thank God she'd downloaded her favourite playlists already. And she'd die before she posted pics of this shrivelled-up place anytime soon. Not when everyone back home was expecting to see Harbour Bridge and Opera House selfies on her feed. Still, she'd ask Jen for the wi-fi details first thing tomorrow.

Wait, what if this place had no internet or wi-fi? She moved around the room trying to find a better spot to make her call, but her bedroom was a verifiable dead zone. Arm stretched out and cell in hand, she covered every corner of the room but had no luck finding a spot with any decent reception. What was this, the *Middle Ages*?

The only time her cell cooperated was when she stood with one foot in the room and the other out the glass doors leading onto the veranda. No data meant there was no way for Maya to check if Emmy was awake and online. It was the middle of the night back home, but her best friend was often up late tweaking her latest baking creation video. She didn't want to wake her but … Maya opened her favourites, scrolled to the Es, and with eyes closed, turned her face towards the cool breeze starting to build outside.

'Maya?' Emmy's groggy voice answered.

Maya winced. 'You were asleep.'

'Yeah, hard to believe at three in the morning.'

Three? Maya winced harder.

'I'm so sorry, Em. I thought you might be working on that raspberry liquorice cake video and I really needed to talk, but I'll call back later when you're—'

'I'm up now.' The soft rustle of bedding travelled down the phone line. 'The place must be unbelievably awesome if you're calling in the middle of the night to tell me.'

'Awesome?' Maya couldn't keep her voice from hitching. 'No, Emmy, it's so far from awesome it's in its own crappy galaxy far, far away.'

'I don't understand. That Sydney baker I follow is always posting gorgeous pics of the city.'

'Sydney probably *is* gorgeous, but I wouldn't know because I'm stuck four hours out of Sydney in some Hicksville backwater!' As soon as the heated words left Maya's mouth, Jen's welcoming face flashed before her eyes and the heat of guilt crept along her cheekbones. Maybe *Hicksville backwater* was a bit harsh, but it described the utter sense of helplessness Maya felt at the way this trip was dying a slow death before it had even started.

'Wait, so if you're not in Sydney, where exactly are you?'

In hell. Or the next best thing … 'A sheep farm.'

Maya slumped against the doorframe then shot bolt upright again, worried she'd lose the little reception she had.

'Sheep farm? Like, with real sheep?'

Maya bit her lip at the confusion in her friend's voice. Emmy— like her parents—had gently encouraged her to take more interest in the planning of this trip. She should have listened.

'I screwed up. I didn't realise there was a Barangaroo in Sydney as well as a Barangaroo *Creek*, which looks to be in the middle of fly-ridden Australian sheep country of all places.'

'Wow, okay. A sheep farm.'

'Yeah, I know.' Maya groaned. 'How could I have messed up this badly, Em? I should have made more effort, paid more attention.' She wanted to slide down to the floor and bury her face in her hands but was too afraid to lose reception.

Emmy made a soothing sound. 'Go easy on yourself. You've had a fair bit on your mind. The funeral, senior year, end of school on top of it all.'

'It's a sheep farm. A *sheep* farm, Em!' She rubbed a hand over her face. 'You know what I'm like with farm animals.'

'I'm sure it'll all work out,' her friend said. 'You never know, you might even enjoy it. Get that real Aussie experience.'

Maya rolled her eyes. Em hadn't been the one walking around with a hoof print on her forehead after *her* first livestock encounter.

'Doubtful. Especially since the host guy seems to have a bullwhip lodged up his butt.'

The bedding rustled on the other end again. Maya could just imagine Emmy sitting up to attention. '*Guy*? Weren't you meant to have a host sister?'

'Yes, but she's had to go help out with some urgent family matter and won't be around for the next six weeks. So I'm stuck with her uppity brother.'

'Uppity how?'

'Uppity as in sending me some undeniable *I wish you were anywhere but here* vibes.'

There were a couple of beats of silence. Thanks to the lack of data, this wasn't their usual video call and Maya had to imagine her friend's expression as she digested this unfortunate slice of information. 'His sister leaving has probably caught him off guard,' she eventually said. 'Maybe he'll mellow with time.'

'Maybe, but I don't have a lot of time. I'm only here for six weeks.' Even though six weeks in this sheep-riddled country seemed like an eternity. 'I need to concentrate on what's important, like how I'm going to tick off the items on my *List*.'

'Totally agree. And I think the farm might actually be handy for a couple of your items.'

'I'm listening.'

'The kangaroo and koala.'

The animals. Of course the first thing Em suggested had to do with blasted animals.

Maya's shoulders slumped. As much as she didn't like the idea, Em was right. 'Cuddling a koala and feeding a kangaroo it is. I'll ask about it as soon as I can.'

Because no matter how much she wanted to give in to the urge to hop on the next plane home, she'd risk animal disasters and put up with surly farmer boys in this fly-ridden corner of the world to complete the items on the *List*.

Chapter Four

Gus gripped the balcony doorframe so hard his nails dug into the old wood. Eavesdropping wasn't his style, but Maya's words floated in on the cool southerly: ... *stuck four hours out of Sydney in some Hicksville backwater ... didn't realise ... Barangaroo Creek ... middle of stinking, fly-ridden Australian sheep country.*

Gus's shower hadn't been anywhere near as long as he'd have liked, but it'd been plenty long for him to reflect on his behaviour since Maya's arrival and come to the shameful conclusion that he'd acted like a total and utter arse. Five minutes ago he'd been ready to apologise; not like the girl could help that his sister had been called away. Five minutes ago he'd been willing to admit Maya was as much a victim as he was of his parents'—scratch that, his *father's*—decision that Gus take over Ruth's role and play host for the next six weeks. Well, five minutes ago he didn't have a bullwhip lodged up his butt.

He pushed away from the balcony doors and prowled over to his drawers in search of a T-shirt. His guilt, along with any intention to apologise, had cooled quicker than the evening air and now crystallised into an icy anger in the pit of his stomach.

Hicksville backwater.

She'd looked completely shell-shocked the moment she'd stepped out of the car. All that curly black hair against her freckle-free face made those big brown eyes pop in a hold-your-breath kinda way. Gus *really* wished he hadn't noticed. He couldn't remember exactly where Ruth had said she was from, but the way she'd half-wilted in the late afternoon heat on the short walk from the car to the house, made Gus doubt it was a place that hit above twenty-five in the summer. That should have been his first warning. Other than that, though, there hadn't been anything to indicate she'd chuck a mega hissy fit at being on a farm.

Her get-up was unassuming enough. Plain red T-shirt, worn-in runners, a surprising lack of makeup ... There really wasn't anything remotely pretentious about the girl. The factory-made fray on her jeans was the only nod her outfit made to any sort of trend or fashion. Then again, Ruth had a similar pair, and she'd bought those at Target, not some fancy designer label store.

So the girl had expected to end up in the city, not the country ... but *Hicksville backwater? Where did she get off?* She'd hardly seen any of the farm or estate. Wherever Maya came from, she wouldn't know that Barangaroo Creek Estate sat on some of the most sought after sheep farming land in the whole country. His parents' Merino stock had won multiple awards and produced first grade wool. Brands like Armani and Gucci and ... and ... He couldn't remember them all, but heaps of well-known designer houses made clothes from their wool. Heaps! *Hicksville backwater. As if!*

Gus gave his hair one more too-rough rub with his towel and looked around for a hairbrush. His eyes fell on the duffle bag and surfboard waiting patiently near his bedroom door, and everything in him stilled. Like Maya, he didn't want to be on the farm—the bag and board a silent reminder.

The irony. Both of them would much rather be in Sydney for the next six weeks, but they were stuck here instead. *Feeding kangaroos and cuddling koalas.* This was a working farm, not some bloody petting zoo. The only thing they cuddled here were hay bales before they hand fed them to the drought-stricken sheep. And now all his well-laid plans were about to go up in dust, just so some spoilt American chick could tick off some stupid clichéd items on a stupid clichéd Aussie list.

Gus raked his hands through his hair and cursed. Stupid hair was already half dry and sticking up at weird angles. *Stuff the hairbrush.*

It wasn't like he was out to impress anyone.

Chapter Five

On the surface, Maya's best friend came across sweet and fluffy—a bit like the baked goods she so loved to create—but Emmy and Maya's friendship ran deeper than the Pacific separating the two friends. She felt awful for waking her, but talking with Emmy had been exactly what Maya needed. Not that she was suddenly happy with where she'd be spending the next six weeks, but Emmy had put things into perspective, reminding Maya why she was here.

She'd unpacked her bag but despite her out-of-whack body clock, Maya was too wired to lie down and rest for a bit like Jen had suggested. A spray of deodorant and a few strokes of her hairbrush later, she stuck her head out the door into the hallway. Thankfully, Gus and his bullwhip were nowhere in sight. She followed the smell of something tomato-and-herb-based down the hallway, hoping it would lead her to the kitchen and Jen. She could really do with a friendly face right now. But it wasn't just Jen she found.

The younger guy sitting at the kitchen table spotted her first. Eyes the same dark brown as Gus's but set in a slightly older—and thankfully friendlier—face.

He smiled at her. 'Hey.'

The man sitting next to him looked up from the magazine in his hands. His smile was tired and weathered but no less friendly. 'Come in. Come in.' He waved her into the kitchen.

'Maya!' Jen stopped whatever she was stirring on the stove. 'Meet Patrick, my eldest, and my husband, Richard. And take a seat. Dinner will be ready soon,' she said, pulling out a chopping board and bread knife.

Maya sat across from Patrick at the well-worn kitchen table. His smile proved her *friendlier* theory.

'So, you're stuck here with us for the next six weeks.'

'Yes, six weeks.' She tried to make it sound like she was looking forward to it, but she'd never been that good at theatre.

Neither Jen nor Richard seemed to pick up on the downturn in Maya's voice; their focus remained on the magazine and stove and pots respectively. Patrick, however, angled his head, curiosity sharpening his eyes.

'First time this far from home?'

Maya nodded.

He waited for more and she sifted through possible responses. She didn't want anything inappropriate to slip out. It wasn't their fault she'd ended up here.

'My first time staying on a farm.' She shifted in her chair. 'I'm more at home tinkering with the cars in my dad's garage than around animals.' Or at least she used to be.

Richard looked at her the way most men of his generation did when she revealed her favourite pastime—like she'd gone and ripped a tear in some age-old gender time-space continuum. Patrick looked surprised, but he didn't act like she'd threatened to remove his manhood with a hidden wrench in her pocket.

Jen placed a steaming bowl of pasta on the table. 'You fix cars?' Her question held more intrigue than surprise.

'I wouldn't say fix. More take apart and put back together and hope for the best.' Michael had been the one good at the fixing part, not so much her.

Patrick nodded, a thoughtful expression on his face. 'Maybe you can help take apart and put back together some of the machinery around here.'

He pushed away from the table but didn't stand. Instead, he rolled around to Maya's side—in his wheelchair.

Maya tried to respond, opened her mouth to tell him that, for her, *fix* meant small things like blocked fuel pumps and spark plugs in need of replacement, but the surprise of seeing someone so young— so *healthy*—in a wheelchair tied knots in her tongue.

If Patrick noticed, he didn't make a thing of it. 'I'm sure Mum told me, but remind me, where are you from?'

'Chicago,' she managed.

'Ah, the windy city,' Richard said, eyes back on his magazine.

Why was that the first thing people thought of? There was so much more to Chicago than the weather. Hiding out at Garfield Park Conservatory on a rainy day. Walking along the 606 at dusk. Places she and Michael would escape to when the noise of the world grew too loud inside their heads. She reached for the comforting coolness of leather on her wrist.

Patrick pulled some plates and cutlery from a sideboard, sat them in his lap, and wheeled himself back to the table. 'So what made you decide on an Australian farm experience?' he asked.

The wave of sadness came out of nowhere, pushing at her ribs, clouding up her eyes. It always happened like this; just when she thought she'd waded through the thickest of the grief, something stupid caught her off guard and threatened to drag her back under. Like Patrick's totally innocent question.

Driven by manners and the desperate need to distract herself, she scooped the pile of cutlery from Patrick's lap as he passed and jumped up to help set the table. She still needed to answer his question.

'The Hemsworth brothers.' As soon as the words were out, heat flooded her face. *The Hemsworth brothers? Really?* She couldn't bring herself to look at Richard or Jen, and definitely not Patrick. Placing the knives and forks completely straight on the table suddenly became all consuming.

'You have the wrong town,' a voice said. A voice Maya was fast finding annoying. 'This here's Barangaroo Creek, not Byron Bay.'

She looked up just as Gus walked into the kitchen. 'No Hemsworths here,' he said, grabbing a piece of cucumber from the salad bowl and popping it into his mouth before carrying it to the table.

'No Hemsworths maybe, but this guy—' Patrick pointed at Gus, '—can knock up a mean looking Thor for you, hammer and all, thanks to his fancy digital animation program.'

Gus threw his brother a dirty look. 'What does that have to do with anything?'

Pat shrugged. 'Just thought maybe Maya might be interested in seeing some of your animations. Didn't you have to do a science task once where you had to come up with a superhero based on a chemical element? Yours was … hold on, don't tell me …' He clicked his fingers in the air, thinking, *thinking* … 'Bromine!' He pointed at Gus, grinning, then turned to Maya as she sat back down beside him. 'His animated hero was this cool guy who could melt and pool under doors and through cracks like that nasty bit of work from *Terminator*. Impressive stuff.' Patrick nodded in Gus's direction, genuinely impressed with his brother's ability.

'Bromine melts at room temperature,' Gus explained, eyes turned down at the table, maybe to hide the sudden smear of pink across his cheeks. 'Anyway, that was back in Year 9. I don't even know if I have it anymore.'

'It was still cool,' Patrick said. 'You've designed some pretty impressive stuff over the years.'

Gus made a noncommittal noise and fished another piece of cucumber out of the salad bowl. He didn't seem to know how to take his brother's praise.

'Waste of time, if you ask me,' Richard said, putting his magazine aside. Maya caught sight of some sort of tractor on the cover. 'A Bromine superhero won't help him when he's out in the paddocks.'

Out of the corner of her eye, Maya saw Gus stiffen. His mouth opened like he was about to say something. He took a breath instead, and reached for the water jug on the table, not saying anything more. But Maya didn't miss the hardening line of his jaw.

'Ignore these two,' Jen said, as she returned with another serving dish filled with a tomato and meat sauce of some sort. The hearty scent of it reminded Maya her last meal had been some time ago and had come inside a small compartmentalised aluminium container. The only good things ever to come in a compartmentalised aluminium container were nuts and bolts, not food.

Her stomach growled. So loudly that four sets of eyes all looked her way.

Maya sucked on her bottom lip. 'Sorry. It's been a while since I've eaten.'

Jen's answering smile was full of understanding. 'Well then, what are we waiting for?' She pushed the bowl of pasta in Maya's direction and waved at her to start serving herself. 'Now, tell us, what are some of the things you're hoping to do while you're here?'

'Yeah, Maya.' Gus reached across the table to pour her a glass of water. 'What are some of your *must-dos* while Down Under?'

Maya looked at Gus across the table. Something in the way he asked his question wasn't sitting right. His tone lacked the edge he'd used with his father, but there was definitely something there.

Maya shifted in her seat and piled a small mountain of pasta onto her plate. 'There are a few things I'd like to do. There's the Opera House and the Harbour Bridge of course, but I'd also like to see some of your wildlife. Kangaroos, koalas, that sort of thing. I also need to eat a piece of Vegemite toast.'

She thought she heard Gus gag, but couldn't be sure; he'd turned to grab some bread from the basket at the other end of the table.

'Oh, and I'd love to play a didgeridoo if possible.'

'Nah-ah. Not possible,' Gus said around a bite of bread.

Maya threw a sceptical glance across the table. 'Why not?'

Gus took his time downing his bread before he answered. 'Playing the didgeridoo is secret men's business,' he finally said. 'Aboriginal culture says women aren't allowed to play it.'

Maya swallowed and looked around the table. 'Is that true?'

Her host mother's expression didn't fill her with confidence.

'Yes and no,' Jen said. 'Some Aboriginal communities have no problem with women playing the instrument in non-ceremonial settings, whereas others are quite opposed to the idea in any setting.' She gave Maya an apologetic look. 'That doesn't stop you from listening to it being played, though.'

But would just listening to it count as completing the item on her List? Maya forced a smile, not wanting to appear ungrateful— she'd worry about this list item later.

'The kangaroos are easy at least,' Patrick offered. 'They're all over the paddocks every dawn and dusk, some of them pretty tame. The koalas on the other hand ...' He pursed his lips, thinking.

'What about the WIRES sanctuary?' Jen asked Gus as she passed Maya the meat sauce. 'They often have a koala or two recovering from an injury or needing relocation. You could give Condo a ring and ask if you could take Maya up later this week once she's settled in.'

The tight line of Gus's mouth told Maya exactly what he thought of *that* idea.

'As for the trip to Sydney, Jen was planning to take you and Gus up one weekend. Maybe even the one coming up,' Richard said. 'That'll cover the Opera House and Bridge, and there's always someone playing a didgeridoo at Circular Quay, so that'll take care of that.' He gave her a self-assured nod before he dug into his dinner.

Patrick held out the salad bowl to Maya. 'There you go, you're all set. You'll have a great time.' She didn't know why, but she almost believed him. Maybe because he'd somehow managed to put her at ease from the moment she'd met him. Why did it have to be Gus that she was stuck with? She'd much rather hang out with Patrick. *He* didn't show any signs of having a bullwhip lodged up his butt.

No point moaning about things she couldn't change. In the end, it didn't matter; tomorrow she'd be one day closer to ticking off the things on her *List*.

She pulled her dinner plate towards her and dug into her meal.

Chapter Six

Gus might have been born on the farm, but he'd never learned to love the early mornings that came with farming life. His father literally bounced into the day, wide awake with the first call of the birds. No rubbing sleep from tired eyes or dragging of heels. Pat wasn't quite as enthusiastic as their father about the five am starts, but even he somehow managed to look alert across the breakfast table each morning.

Gus stumbled out of bed like he suffered from permanent jetlag.

Normally it took a plate of fried eggs and his usual cup of coffee—two sugars, easy on the milk—to shed his morning fog. Not this morning though. He jerked wide awake when he saw Maya standing next to his mother in the kitchen, sipping what he assumed was a cup of coffee. She gave him a tentative smile over the rim of her mug. Make that *his* mug. *Jurassic Park*, limited edition. Maybe his body went on high alert because she had her hands on one of his prized possessions—his mother should have known better than to let her use it—or maybe it was the smile itself.

'Morning,' he mumbled, heading for the coffee. There was something to be said for easing into the day in a half fog. At least then he wouldn't be so annoyingly aware of their new house guest. What was she even wearing? Hadn't overalls been read the riot act by the fashion police? Although, he had to admit the distressed denim cut-offs looked kinda cute on her. Showed off her legs.

Gus shook his head. He wasn't interested in Maya's legs.

'Finally.' His mother turned his way, an unimpressed frown stamped across her brow, but she let her usual *you're up late again* lecture slide. Maybe because Maya was still watching keenly over the rim of her—*his*—mug. He should have been relieved. Instead, he felt rubbed the wrong way. What was *wrong* with him?

'We were thinking it'd be nice for Maya to tag along with you this morning. That way you can introduce her to the farm, you know, show her around.'

Show her around to the nearest bus stop. Judging by his mother's expression, that suggestion wouldn't go down too well.

Gus answered in grunt form. Immature, *yes,* but the day was not starting well. He downed his coffee and grabbed a banana. Thanks to his late start, he didn't have enough time for a proper breakfast before he headed out to the top paddock. No matter; his appetite had disappeared anyway.

'So what exactly are we doing today?'

Maya's question caught Gus by surprise. She'd been quiet all the way to the shed. Something he couldn't blame her for, since he hadn't exactly been Mr. Sunshine back in the kitchen.

'Feeding sheep.'

'Don't they eat grass?'

'Not when there's no grass to eat.' He slapped his thigh, calling Ralph away from her. Maya stiffened every time the dog so much as sniffed her way. 'We haven't had any decent rain in months.' He'd have to feed the ewes and weaners every day until then. Not a prospect he was looking forward to.

'A pickup?' Maya looked past him once they stepped into the shed.

Gus eyed her over the roof of the car. 'That'd be a ute, yeah. What did you expect?'

'Um, I don't know… horses?'

Gus grinned at the creep of pink across Maya's face. But her suggestion wasn't all that left field. 'Horses are used mainly for mustering, although we use cars and quad bikes for that here. Handfeeding is done with utes or trucks. Easier to pull one of these with a ute.' He slapped the side of the trailer feeder at the back of the ute, then pulled himself up on the side to check how full it was. He'd need to top it up tomorrow, but it was enough to feed the mob today.

He motioned for Maya to hop in the cab of the ute, then climbed in himself and whistled for Ralph to jump in between them.

'You disappointed about the horses?' he asked, cranking the engine.

A nervous laugh burst through the cabin. 'No. Relieved. I wouldn't know the first thing about horses.'

He waited for her to tell him she didn't know the first thing about sheep either, but she kept quiet, eyes darting between the countryside through the window and Ralph perched between them on the bench seat.

Might as well give her some background about the farm. 'Barangaroo Creek Estate sits on about six thousand hectares of land. My great grandfather started out with a herd of a couple of hundred. Now we have close to a thousand head of sheep and about a hundred head of cattle.'

Her throat bobbed on a not-so-subtle swallow at the mention of *cattle*.

She cleared her throat and looked over at Gus. 'That's a lot of sheep. What about other animals? I thought I saw some alpacas near the house.'

'Yeah, Al Pacino and Armani.'

'Seriously?' Maya gave him a sceptical look. 'Do they strut around the paddock in suits or something?'

Gus slid her a sideways glance. 'No, but they do guard our lambs and chooks.'

Maya's confused frown brought a smile to Gus's lips. 'From

foxes. Alpacas are fiercely protective. They make great guard animals.' He stopped the ute. 'Wait here a sec.' He hopped out to open the gate to the next paddock, then hopped back into the car.

'Other than the alpacas, we have half a dozen chooks and four sheep dogs.' Ralph barked as though to remind Gus of the most important animal on the farm. 'And then there's Ralph, of course.'

On cue, the dog licked Gus's face. Maya leaned away, giving the mutt a wide berth.

'Let me guess, you're not that good with dogs either?' He gently pushed Ralph away and wiped his cheek on his shoulder.

She shrugged. 'I've never had a dog or any kind of pet. Animals and me ...' She clamped her bottom lip between her teeth. 'Not a good combination.'

'And a farm stay fits into this how?' Gus raised a brow.

Maya crossed her arms. 'Maybe I thought it was time to challenge myself.'

Gus's brow inched higher still.

'Okay, fine. I didn't really want to do a farm stay.' Her shoulders slumped and she looked out at the empty paddock they were crossing like it was Mars and she was a stranded Matt Damon, doomed to eat potatoes until she was rescued from her red and dusty fate. 'I wanted to go to the city.'

'Where it's easier to complete your *must-do* list, you mean?'

'Well, yeah.'

Her honesty stung. 'There's more to experiencing Australia than koalas and kangaroos.'

'I'm sure there is, but this is something I have to do.'

'You know that list you rattled off last night is about as clichéd as taking a photo with Mickey at Disney Land or calling Chicago the windy city.' Gus stopped the ute at another gate.

Eyes wide, Maya looked at him like he'd violated her thoughts. She opened the door and slid out of the ute.

Okay, maybe that last comment was too much.

He made to follow her—if his parents found out he'd ticked her off there'd be hell to pay—but then he saw the paddock gate. Maya had opened it and was waiting for him to drive through. She wasn't chucking a hissy fit like he'd assumed.

He drove through the gate and watched her latch it in the rearview mirror.

He cleared his throat when she hopped back in the ute. 'Thanks. I didn't mean to, um, you know, offend you with the list thing.'

She shrugged, but didn't look at him. 'I wasn't offended.'

Gus swallowed his snort. 'Right, so that I-wanna-punch-you look just now was for one of the sheep?'

The side-eye she threw him was all the answer he needed.

'The list might be clichéd but it's important to me.' She wound a strand of hair around her finger and tucked it behind her ear. 'You wouldn't understand.'

Sure. Because we're all backward in this Hicksville backwater.

Gus drove on in silence.

'There are … so many.' Maya leaned forward, looking out over the ewes and lambs in the paddock.

'That's only half of them. There's another lot over there.' Gus pointed to a second paddock further up the hill where a clump of sheep clustered near the gate. 'You think you can drive this through while I keep an eye on the mob near the front here, so they don't sneak out?'

Maya eyed the steering wheel suspiciously, then looked at the dash in front of her. Everything was on the wrong side to what she was used to, which must have been a bit daunting.

He took pity on her. 'You know what, I think I'll be good—'

'Okay.' She cut him off with a nod. One that looked a lot more confident than her expression led him to believe she was. She didn't even give him a chance to argue; she'd jumped out of the car and was circling the front to the driver's side.

Gus climbed out, Ralph close on his heels.

Maya hopped in. 'Gas is on the left, yes?'

Gus frowned. Maybe this wasn't such a good idea.

'Never mind.' Maya grabbed the steering wheel. 'I've got this.' She nodded again like she was trying to convince herself. The girl was nothing if not committed.

Gus gave her a tight smile. 'Accelerator on the *right*, brake on the left.' At least it wasn't a stick shift. That'd just add an unnecessary complication.

He turned for the gate before he could change his mind. With a little encouragement from him and a few enthusiastic barks from Ralph, the ewes moved out of the way, lambs in tow.

Gus waved Maya into the paddock. She rolled the ute through the gate. Slowly, but without a hitch. Once she was fully inside, he latched the gate and made for the driver's side of the ute.

He opened the door and waited for Maya to climb out. She didn't move.

'Can I drive a bit more? I've almost got the hang of this right side steering business.'

This was the last thing Gus was expecting. The feeding trough was at the other end of the paddock, but what damage could she do?

'Yeah, um, sure,' Gus said. 'Just hang on a sec. I'll jump back in.' At least that way he could grab the wheel if she was in danger of running over any sheep.

Surprisingly, the ride was uneventful. It was slow—the paddock was full of sheep—but Maya manoeuvred the ute through the throng of animals with serious concentration. She pulled the ute to a stop alongside the feeding troughs and cranked the handbrake. Gus glanced at her with a new set of eyes; Maya all capable behind the wheel of a ute. He scratched his jaw ... *This could be kinda useful.*

'So, what now?' She turned to face him, a strange mix of expectation and apprehension widening her eyes.

Gus leaned across her lap and turned off the ignition. 'Now we feed the sheep,' he said, climbing out of the car.

Maya gingerly followed him through the mob of sheep to the back of the ute, where he pulled a couple of buckets from the tray of the car. 'Here.' He handed one to her and walked around to the back of the trailer. 'Grain comes out of here.' As soon as he opened the feeder and the grain flowed into the trough, the ewes jostled around them for prime position. 'Fill your bucket and spread the feed out evenly across the trough,' he told Maya holding his bucket high, so the sheep couldn't get to it. 'When this one's full, we'll move the ute to the next one.'

The way she scrunched up her nose, he half expected her to object, but she nodded and stuck her bucket under the feeder. They spent the next ten minutes filling up the several metre-long troughs, then drove on into the next paddock to repeat the process.

Gus watched her out of the corner of his eye for a bit. With her dirt-smeared cutoffs and chaotic dark curls sticking to her sweat-streaked brow, she almost passed for a local. *If* you could convince yourself the frown on her face was one of concentration and not growing frustration. What really gave it away was her constant swatting at the flies like they were about to eat her face or the way she jumped every time a sheep brushed up against her. Which was, like, every couple of seconds.

'Right, that's this lot done,' Gus said, motioning Maya back to the ute. 'That should keep them happy until tomorrow.'

'Tomorrow?' Maya gaped at him. 'You mean we have to do all this again tomorrow?'

'Yep, and every day after that for as long as you're here, most likely.'

Her face fell. There was no other way to describe it. All her features shifted down by a few millimetres. And that was without him telling her there were another dozen or so paddocks that were on feed rotation every three days. At this rate she wouldn't last a week, let alone six.

Gus's mind raced back to his room, to the surfboard sitting against his wall, to the duffle bag bulging with dreams that he'd never get to unpack. He'd last the six weeks. He'd last the rest of his life. He had no choice.

He sighed. 'Come on,' he said, opening the ute's passenger door for her. 'It's almost lunch. Let's get going before it gets too hot.'

Maya went to climb into the ute, but froze and shrieked, scrambling backwards and almost knocking Gus over in her attempt to get away from the car.

'Snake! There's a snake!'

She pointed frantically at the ground near the ute's door with one hand while her other gripped his upper arm hard enough to cut off circulation.

On instinct, Gus shuffled them both back from the car, then zeroed in on the cracked rough ground. *There, a scaly brown tail in a clump of dried grass.* He tensed. The area was known for Eastern Browns. If this was one, it was juvenile, but even at that age the little hissers were dangerous.

He swallowed, held his breath, stepped a little closer, heart *rat-a-tat-ing* in his ears. A little closer still … and he smiled. 'It's only a squeaker.'

'A *what?*' Maya didn't sound reassured.

'A striped legless lizard.' He bent to pick it up. Sure enough, the little fellow had distinct ear openings and a tell-tale yellow throat. No Eastern Brown, thank God. 'Haven't seen one of these in years. Cute little critters. Here, take look.' He held out the ruler-length lizard to Maya.

Hands up and palms out, she took another quick step backwards. 'Keep the squealer away from me.'

'Squeaker,' Gus corrected. 'They're harmless. Honest.'

But Maya wouldn't go anywhere near the little reptile.

'Why squeakers?' she asked as Gus bent to deposit the lizard in a patch of brush near the fence.

Gus threw her a deadpan look over his shoulder. 'Cause of the way tourists *squeak* when they come across one.'

Her eyes widened in mock surprise. 'With material like that, I'm floored you haven't got your own YouTube channel.'

Mouth twitching, Gus stood and brushed his hands off on his shorts. 'Been checking me out online, have you?'

Maya's face flushed, but Gus was pretty sure she hadn't done any online checking. Otherwise she'd know he *did* have a YouTube channel.

'The lizards make a squeaking noise when they're upset, so … squeakers,' Gus said, turning back to the ute.

'All the more reason not to go anywhere near them,' Maya muttered.

Gus shook his head. *Spooked by harmless sheep and scared of baby lizards. What would the girl do when she encountered some of the creepier wildlife on the farm?*

There hadn't been any incidents for a while, but a few years back Pat found a nest of snake eggs in the tractor shed. Three dozen potential Eastern Browns. Even Dad's face had paled when he realised what they were dealing with.

More likely, though, would be a face-to-face with a huntsman. The spiders were everywhere, and knowing they were as harmless as they were hairy didn't stop Gus's pulse from tripping over itself whenever he saw one. Those blighters could jump and had no concept of personal space. Only last week he'd ended up with one on his back after sweeping out the wool shed. *Shudder*; he still had bruises on his back from whacking himself with the broom to get the bloody thing off him.

Gus could just imagine Maya screaming down the house after spotting a fist-sized huntsman sitting all casual on the bathroom mirror, or scampering along a wall, or even dropping onto her face in the middle of the night. *Double shudder.* That kind of nightmare wasn't unheard of. She'd be out of the house faster than a sheep dog to a muster, probably willing to leg it all the way to Sydney so she could catch the earliest plane back to—

Gus straightened like he'd been poked with a cattle prod. He glanced over at Maya. She'd climbed into the ute and, face pale, arms crossed, waited for him to get in the car.

Slowly, the corners of his lips tugged north. Maya might have her list, with its koalas and kangaroos and didgeridoos, but a different kind of list was forming in Gus's mind. One that would have Maya booking the next flight to the windy city.

And Gus heading for Sydney in no time.

Chapter Seven

The moment the pickup—*or ute or whatever*—pulled into the shed, Maya jumped out and made straight for the house.

'Hey, what's the hurry?' Gus called after her. 'No lizards here. I promise.' She didn't need to turn around to see the smirk on his face. It boomed in his voice.

'I need the bathroom.' A lie. What she needed was a cold shower to wash all the dirt and dust and sheep smell off. But more so, she needed to be left alone for a bit so she could settle her rattled nerves and maybe lick the wounds on her battered ego.

A lizard. How was I meant to know that thing had been a lizard? It had no legs. It looked like a snake! Okay, so maybe a small snake, but any snake in this hellish corner of the world could be deadly, and she wasn't a fan of snakes at the best of times.

Inside her room, she fell onto her bed and dragged the pillow over her head. It shut out the light but did little to block out her mortification. She must have looked so stupid, screaming and carrying on like some kindergartener spooked by a bug. She wasn't the type to go all *save me, save me* whenever she saw a rat or cockroach or even a spider, but snakes were on a completely different creep-out level.

And as if she'd be looking him up online! Okay, the prospect of a host brother instead of a host sister might have resulted in some online stalking and possibly less skimming of the information booklet for this trip. Maybe, if this place wasn't the Black Hole of internet reception …

The thought brought Maya out from under her pillow and reaching for her cell phone. Jen hadn't exactly filled her with confidence when she handed over the wi-fi password along with words like *patchy* and *temperamental* this morning, but Maya lived in hope. The dodgy network allowed her to connect easily enough. She opened Instagram, then coiled several errant strands of hair around her finger and shoved them back under her hair elastic while she waited for the app to load.

A knock on the door made Maya jump.

'You alright in there?' Gus's voice was full of concern. Probably all fake.

'I'm fine.' She'd be better if he went away.

'Okaaay. Heads up then, I'm taking you to the animal sanctuary after lunch so you can … you know … cuddle your koala.'

Maya heard the eye roll that she couldn't see through the closed door. Well, he could shove his eye roll where he kept his bullwhip. Who cared what uptight Farmer Boy thought anyway. As long as she ticked off the items on her *List*, he could roll his eyes down the hallway for all she cared.

She turned off her cell—Instagram still hadn't loaded—hopped off the bed and opened the door. And paused. Gus wasn't smirking or looking cocky. He just peered at her from under raised brows. If he was waiting for her to gush with thanks, he'd be standing there a while. It wasn't like he was taking her to the sanctuary out of the goodness of his heart.

'Do I have time for a shower?' she asked.

Gus glanced over his shoulder at the ajar bathroom door, then back at her. 'Sure.'

He smiled and turned for his own bedroom down and across the hall. Maya watched his broad shoulders until he disappeared through his door. She frowned; there was something about the way his lips had twitched that she didn't trust.

Chapter Eight

'So what kind of animals does this sanctuary look after?' Maya asked as Gus pulled the ute onto the road heading to Doranco.

It was a short trip. Thank the stars for that. He wasn't all that keen on being stuck in a confined space with Maya for an extended period of time.

'All sorts,' Gus said. 'Flying foxes, possums, gliders. Animals get dehydrated in long stretches of hot weather. Hot roads and roofs burn paws. And then there's the bushfires, forcing wildlife to flee habitats, wreaking all sorts of devastation. Oh, and people often call WIRES when someone finds a snake in their house.'

Gus snuck a look at Maya to see if his words had hit their mark. *Yup, bullseye.* Wide-eyed and stiff as a fence post. He smiled to himself.

'WIRES?' she asked once the shock of snakes in houses had worn off.

'Wildlife Information, Rescue and Education Service.'

She nodded a silent *ah*. 'So what's the likelihood of a koala being at the refuge this time of year?'

'No bushfires at the moment.' Good thing, too. If there were, he'd have no chance of getting away for his *holiday*. 'But it's been hot for weeks, so they have a fair few animals they're looking after. A koala included.' Gus had called Condo earlier to make sure the trip wasn't wasted. In more ways than one.

'I don't get it. You said yourself, animals aren't your thing.' He frowned over at Maya. 'Why would you even want to cuddle a koala?'

She peered across at him all quiet and serious like she was weighing up if she could trust him with the answer. 'It's not about what I want,' she eventually said. 'It's about doing what's right.'

What did that even mean? He opened his mouth to prod some more when his phone rang. He pressed *talk* on the dash console a split second before he realised the only familiar thing about the number on the display: the Sydney area code.

'Hello?'

'Am I speaking with Gus Robertson? I'm calling from the Art faculty at Sydney University.'

Oh no. Gus's gaze flicked across to Maya. How much of this conversation did he want her to hear? She might repeat something to his parents, which could get messy. Very messy. *Of all the times for my phone to get decent reception …* He had to deflect.

'Yes, Gus Robertson here. But I'm driving right now, so it's a little difficult for me to speak. Can I call you back?'

Out of the corner of his eye, he caught Maya frown. The ute had Bluetooth, so he could talk handsfree. There was no real reason he couldn't take the call.

'Certainly. In case you're wondering, it's in regards to the CGI summer school you enrolled in.'

Gus sucked in a breath. He hadn't been wondering, but judging by the curious expression on Maya's face, she now bloody well was.

'Right, sure, thanks. I'll call back as soon as I'm off the road.'

Gus hung up before the woman said something else that sent Maya's eyebrows climbing up her forehead.

Keep quiet. Concentrate on your driving. With any luck, she wouldn't ask any questions.

A guy could dream.

'You're enrolled in a summer school in Sydney?'

Gus rolled his eyes—of course she'd ask questions.

'*Was* enrolled.' A half truth. Technically his enrolment was still active. Although he suspected the phone call just now meant his time was running out.

'For the whole summer?'

He threw her a quick look. He couldn't figure out if the shaky note in her voice was worry or excitement.

'It doesn't matter. It's not happening anymore, so no point talking about it.'

Say something else. Change the subject. 'When I rang ahead to see about your koala, they told me they had a couple of flying foxes and an echidna they're looking after at the moment. You ever seen an echidna? They're funny-looking things, but real cute.' She should have one of those on her corny bucket list.

Maya nodded. 'It all makes sense now.'

'What?' Gus frowned so hard, it sent an ache across his forehead. 'That echidnas are cute?'

'No.' The note of worry or excitement or whatever he'd previously heard in Maya's voice was gone. Replaced by quiet conviction. 'The reason for your sub-zero welcome when I arrived.'

Gus cringed. He didn't need a reminder of his sub-par behaviour. It was making him question what he was about to do. He turned to check his right side-view mirror. Not because he really needed to, but so Maya wouldn't spot the guilt pulling at his features.

'You were enrolled in this summer school, and now you're not going because of me.' It wasn't a question.

Gus could have continued lying, trying to convince her she had it all wrong. Problem was, he didn't think she'd buy it. She might have had the most clichéd Aussie *must-do* list ever, but even in the short time he'd spent with her, Gus could tell the girl was no fool.

'I'm sorry,' she said, before he had a chance to say anything himself. 'If I'd known your sister was going to be away, I would have asked to be sent somewhere else.'

Yeah, the city. But even though he knew she didn't want to be anywhere near a sheep farm, there was genuine remorse in her voice for having mucked up his plans.

'It's not your fault,' he said, meaning it. 'We didn't even know that Ruth wouldn't be here until only a couple of days ago.'

'Well, I'm sorry anyway. I know what it's like when things don't turn out the way you expect them to.' Her voice had gone all faint and distant. She looked out the window, something big, something important, pulling her into the past.

They drove in welcomed silence for the next few minutes, Maya watching the landscape whizz past, Gus keeping his eyes fixed on the road ahead. It wasn't until he spotted the *Welcome to Doranco* sign that Maya spoke again.

'So, a CGI course as in special effects for movies and stuff?'

Gus sighed. But really, there'd been next to no chance she would drop it. He snuck a sideways look at her. 'Yeah, among other things.'

Maya pursed her lips. 'Interesting.'

'Interesting?' Gus cocked a brow. 'How?'

A shrug. 'I don't know. You just don't look like the type who'd enjoy sitting behind a computer all day.'

Gus smiled. Now he got it. 'You mean like a computer geek?'

Her eyes widened a smidge like she'd been caught out. Gus stopped the car at a set of lights and looked pointedly at Maya. 'Well, you don't look like someone who'd enjoy tinkering under the hood of a car either.'

Maya's gaze briefly dropped to her hands. She brushed her thumbs over her short fingernails before sliding both hands under her thighs.

'Touché,' she said.

The lights turned green. Gus shook this head as he turned into the next street. The girl spent her spare time fiddling with greasy car parts and yet used words like *touché*. She was the one who was interesting. A contradiction. A little like a farmer's son who spent his spare time creating art on computer screens. Gus shifted in his seat at the comparison.

'We say *fair call* around here.' He smiled across at Maya, the need to lighten the mood suddenly strong.

'Fair call, then.' She gave him a smile in return. A cautious one, corners of her lips tugging up slowly, the shadow of a dimple hiding in the cushion of her cheek. He didn't mind seeing it, he realised.

'And is this computer graphic …' Her brows pulled together. 'What does CGI stand for exactly?'

'Computer generated imagery,' he said. *Am I really having this conversation with this girl?*

'Right, so computer generated imagery, is that what you'll be studying at uni next year?'

Maya's question slapped the smile right off Gus's face. 'No.' The word came out short and sharp. Then he saw Maya's expression, all taken aback and off kilter, and he felt, well, like a dick.

'So the summer school, that was just for a bit of fun?' she asked.

Gus shoved fidgety fingers into his hair and scratched his scalp. 'It's … complicated.'

Slowly, Maya nodded, lips mouthing a silent 'okay'. He had no idea what she was thinking. He was just grateful she wasn't asking anymore questions. A couple of beats of silence later she found her voice again.

'I really like all the special effects in all those end-of-the-world movies. You know, the ones where whole cities are swallowed by a mammoth tidal wave.' She swept her arm in front of her in an over-dramatic gesture. 'Or the *Jurassic Park* movies. Those dinosaurs look so real! Knowing how to create stuff like that would be pretty cool.'

'It's not just about cinema special effects.' There was so much more to CGI than what people saw at the movies. 'CGI is used in forensics, medicine, architecture and a whole heap of other fields as well.' Which was why he really wanted to take part in at least some of the summer school program. There was so much he didn't know.

'What field interests you the most?'

He'd thought many hours about this and had always come to the same conclusion. 'I wouldn't mind exploring all the fields—they're interesting in different ways—but if I had to choose just one, then, yeah—' he flicked her a sheepish look, '—it'd be creating virtual worlds and larger-than-life creatures.'

The field his father was least likely to approve of, because what practical function did art serve anyway?

'Okay, movies. Quality of plot lines aside, which ones are your favourites when it comes to special effects?'

His grin was instant. 'Some of your end-of-the-world movies like *Geostorm* and *2012*. Then there are the classics like *The Matrix* and the *Terminator* movies, but *Kong: Skull Island* would have to come close to my number one. The size of the creature meant lots of close ups and the detail in those scenes …' He shook his head. 'I've watched docos about the making of that movie. They added every hair and wrinkle and imperfection on Kong's body by hand. Every hair and wrinkle.'

He turned to catch Maya's reaction and wasn't disappointed. Eyes wide, head slowly nodding, she looked duly impressed.

'I want to do that … create something fantastical out of code, and pixels, and imagination, and make people believe the unbelievable.' He heard the frustrated longing in his voice a fraction too late. Not wanting Maya to see it mirrored in his eyes, he snapped his head to the road.

'I don't get it,' she said. 'You sound like you absolutely dig this stuff. It'd make sense to go and study it. Make a career out of something you love.'

Yes! A thousand times yes! It made perfect sense. Except, it also didn't. Not when there was a farm to run and Gus was the last man standing.

Beside him, Maya was still turned his way, waiting for an answer. He couldn't give her one. He barely knew her. She was only here for

45

six weeks, hopefully even less. Why should he trust her with this part of his life? It wasn't like she'd be able to change anything.

He gritted his teeth and pulled into the Doranco WIRES driveway.

'We're here,' he said, shutting off the engine along with any further discussion on the topic.

Chapter Nine

Maya frowned at Gus's back as he climbed out of the ute. Maybe she shouldn't have pressed him on the whole CGI thing? She didn't regret it, though. Not when Gus's face had lit up like a flame torch, losing that uptight expression.

The skin under the leather band on her wrist itched. Instinctively, she went to twist it, but balled her fingers into a fist instead.

She knew all about not making any plans, about not doing something she loved.

She scrambled out of the ute and followed Gus to the animal refuge entrance.

As soon as Gus opened the door, Ralph darted inside and disappeared through a doorway behind the information desk marked *office*.

'Incoming!' Gus called.

'Ralphster!' Maya heard a guy's voice over the dog's enthusiastic yapping. 'Good to see you too, boy! Now, get down.'

The owner of the voice came through the office door with a bunch of leafy tree branches in his arms and an over-excited Ralph jumping around his calves.

Gus shook his head. 'I swear, that dog likes you better than me.'

'That's cause I give him the discipline he craves.' The guy shifted his tree branches into the crook of one arm so he could stretch the other one Maya's way. 'Name's Condo. You must be Maya.' His large brown eyes smiled a welcome in his tan face. 'I hear you're looking to cuddle a koala?'

'Yes.' Maya looked down at the dog, fighting a rising heat in her cheeks. By his tone, Condo hadn't been teasing. Coming from someone else, though, her request to cuddle a koala sounded ridiculous somehow.

She quashed her discomfort and squared her shoulders, reminding herself why she was doing this. 'Thanks for making it possible.'

Condo rubbed the back of his neck. 'Technically, only staff are meant to handle the wildlife, so you can't tell anyone about this, okay?'

Maya shook her head. 'Wait, I don't want to get you into any trouble.'

'It'll be fine.' Condo's smile spread across his face again. 'Just got to make it a quick cuddle.' He jiggled the leafy branches in his arms. 'I was about to feed the little fella. Come on through.'

Gus shrugged and waved for Maya to follow Condo down a hallway. Ralph trotted ahead of everyone like he owned the place, but when they reached what Maya assumed to be the back door of the building, Gus put Ralph on a leash and tied him to a hallway table. 'Sorry, buddy, you've got to stay here.'

The Jack Russell whined.

'He'll stress the animals,' Gus explained, giving the dog a consolatory scratch under the collar.

The large yard was filled with different sized animal enclosures. Half looked empty. In others, birds squawked or reptiles sunned themselves.

In a centre enclosure, a sleepy grey marshmallow of a koala sat in the fork of a lopped-off tree. The curled-up grey ball made Maya smile despite her nervousness.

'Maya, meet Fraser.' Condo opened the enclosure latch. He spread the leaves he'd been carrying out across one of the thicker tree branches and the koala stirred to life. Seeing lunch was served, he padded over to the leafy meal.

Maya stepped back a little from the enclosure. She was wary and didn't want to startle the animal. 'How did he end up here?' she asked.

'Got trampled by cattle at a nearby farm.' Condo rubbed Fraser behind one ear, something the koala seemed to enjoy. He leaned into the touch even as he continued to munch on the eucalyptus leaves. 'The stampede killed his mother and this poor little guy ended up with a broken leg and internal bleeding. We didn't think he'd pull through, but he's a fighter.'

All blissed out on his leaves, Fraser looked more like a furry couch potato than a fighter.

'Condo's been looking after him for a couple of months now,' Gus said, coming to stand beside her. 'He'll eventually be released back into the bush.'

'Not yet, though,' Condo said. 'He's not ready.'

Gus chuckled. 'Or maybe you're not ready?'

'Maybe.' Condo's smile confirmed Gus's theory. 'He's going to be hard to say goodbye to. Wanna hold him?' he asked Maya.

She hesitated but nodded. She was nervous about touching the animal, but curious, too. Would his fur be as soft as it looked?

Maya edged closer.

Fraser didn't so much as blink when Condo reached fully into the enclosure and picked him up. As long as he had some leaves to munch, he was a happy fur ball.

'No sudden movements.' Condo gently placed Fraser in Maya's arms. 'And watch his claws. They're sharp.'

Maya froze to the spot, the smell of cough drops and something sharper, more pungent, suddenly plunged her into another koala enclosure in another place and time.

'Will you look at that funky face, munching away without a care in the world.' Michael had nudged her, grin wide on his face. 'Think they'll let me hold him?'

They hadn't. The koala had been on loan to Lincoln Park under the strictest conditions. Passing him around the zoo visitors was a definite no.

'I think he likes you.'

At Gus's voice, Maya blinked the memory of her brother's face away. 'It's the meal he likes rather than me.' She focused on the warm weight of the animal in her arms to anchor her in the present. Fraser's fur was woolly on the outer layer and softer where she sunk her fingertips further in. Unlike his paws, which were surprisingly rough and leathery as he clutched her upper arm.

The animal's face fascinated Maya like it had Michael. His bulbous black nose dominated, almost swallowing his much smaller brown button eyes. Add the big bushy ears and white chin markings, and you had an odd-looking creature—*odd, but also ... cute*.

'My cell phone is in my back pocket,' Maya said to Gus. 'Could you take a photo?'

Gus's gaze flicked to the back of her shorts, then back up again. 'How about I use my own phone and just send you the pic,' he said, pulling his cell out already. 'Say "cheesy must-do list".'

'How about you just take the photo and keep the commentary to yourself?'

'Touché,' Gus said, with a mock bow.

Maya sent him her best *you're-not-funny* look, settled her feature into a smile and tried to relax for the camera.

Gus took a few shots while Fraser remained oblivious to all the fuss.

One *must-do* list item down, six more to go.

Maya was starting to feel marginally better about ending up in Australia's version of Hicksville.

A howl drew their attention away from the koala to the back door.

'Ralph.' Gus tucked his phone away. 'I'll go settle him down while you show Maya some of the other animals.'

Condo eased Fraser out of Maya's arms and placed him back in his enclosure. 'While you're in there, there's a small cage behind the front counter for you. It's got the blue—'

'Echidna!' Gus turned suddenly. Eyes wide with urgency, he pointed at Condo. 'Show her the echidna,' he said, then he disappeared back into the building.

This echidna better be something special.

Her doubt must have shown on her face, because Condo's expression turned all animated. 'The echidna *is* pretty cool. Want to see it?'

Maya nodded. 'Okay.' She was here, and now that she had her obligatory mugshot with a koala, she might as well. Bring on the echidna!

The echidna *was* pretty cool. Bit like the love child of a hedgehog and an anteater.

'Harriet was hit by a car and ended up with a broken beak,' Condo said.

'How long before she can be released?'

'Another couple of weeks and she should be good to go.' Condo's smile was sad around the edges.

'You get attached to them, don't you?'

He didn't have to think long about his answer. 'Yeah, I do. But I know they'll be happiest back home where they belong. You know the saying, if you love something set it free. If it comes back to you it was meant to be, or something like that.'

'And have any of them come back to you?'

He sighed, all dramatic. 'I pour all this attention and care into them, nurse them to health, but no, none of them have loved me enough to come back.'

'Tragic.'

'I know, right?'

They both grinned.

Gus came back while Condo was showing Maya the flying fox.

'Ralph okay?' Maya asked.

Gus nodded. 'Almost forgot, these are for you.' He handed Condo a large carton of eggs.

'Thanks. I'll pass these onto Mum,' he said, leading them around the side of the building to where the ute was parked. 'So Ruth's gone for the whole summer holidays?'

'Yeah, real pain that.' Gus's step faltered. He glanced Maya's way. 'Not because, you know …' he waved a hand in Maya's direction, '… because Ruth was meant to be the one to look after … never mind.' He shoved his hand in his pocket and looked straight ahead. Maya fought a fresh wave of guilt at keeping him from his Sydney plans.

Thankfully, Ralph came racing from round the back of the ute at that moment and jumped into the car's cabin.

'Thanks for letting me meet Fraser and all the other animals,' Maya said, climbing into the car behind the dog.

'Anytime,' Condo said. 'Enjoy the rest of your stay in Barangaroo Creek.'

'I will.' Not a complete lie. Holding Fraser had been less traumatic than she'd thought, maybe even … enjoyable. She really should give the farm, her stay—and Gus—a fair chance.

Ralph snuck his head under her arm. She went to pull away but forced herself to stop and pat the dog on the head. If she could hold a koala, she could pat a damn dog.

He nudged closer, tongue lolling dangerously near her face. 'You lick me and this is the last pat I ever give you.'

She swore he smiled up at her. *The nerve!*

Gus climbed into the car. 'You ready to head back?'

'Yeah. I'm ready.'

And maybe Maya was ready for more. For a clean slate. A fresh start. A whole different attitude towards Barangaroo Creek.

Chapter Ten

'How heavy do you think Fraser was?'

Gus looked across the ute at Maya. Her eyes were alight with curiosity; her whole face open with genuine interest instead of the usual barely veiled horror that coated her features. Something like guilt pooled in the pit of his stomach as an image of the cage he'd tucked away at the back of the ute flashed in his mind.

'Three, maybe four kilos,' he said. 'When he first came into the refuge he'd been a scrawny runt, all skin and bones. Condo's fattened him up nicely. Koalas have a rep for being lazy, overweight animals, but they're not. They sleep lots to conserve energy.'

Maya nodded. 'I didn't expect him to be so lean underneath all that fur.'

The entire way home they'd been chatting like this. About the refuge. About the other animals. About how Condo's love for critters started with him saving cicadas back in preschool. Maya looked like she was finally enjoying herself. Which made Gus feel like a royal bastard for what he planned to do ... to get rid of her.

Focus. This is your one *chance—your* last *chance—to do what you love.*

Wasn't Maya the one who said it made sense for him to study what he loved? Well, he couldn't do a full university degree, but he could do the summer school. Once Maya got over the initial shock, she'd understand and hopefully forgive him. Hopefully.

Gus shifted in his seat. The possibility that Maya might well forgive him for what was pretty much unforgivable made him feel worse, not better about his plan.

By the time evening rolled around, he'd almost convinced himself his plan was justified. It made sneaking into Maya's room marginally more acceptable.

Maya's feet padding to the bathroom was his cue. Slowly, he edged her bedroom door open and deposited the small cage on the floor. He paused to take stock of the room: bed was made, clothes stacked neatly on the wardrobe shelves, no piles of dirty laundry anywhere. Unlike his sister, who owned the world's largest floordrobe, this girl was tidy.

So, where to deposit his little surprise for greatest impact … His eyes fell on the bed. Could he? It was the most effective but also a bit, well … nasty. What if she had a panic attack? Or worse, a heart attack? Dislike of animals aside, she didn't strike him as highly strung, but the brain had a way of screwing you over in a stressful situation.

He glanced at his not-so-little friend sitting patiently inside the cage. 'No guarantee you'll stay under the bed covers anyway, is there?' The critter flashed a glimpse of his trademark blue in reply.

Gus blew out a breath between tight lips and heaved the cage onto the bed. He was reaching for the cage door when a ding drew his eyes to the bedside table. A text flashed up on Maya's phone. Great, now he could add 'reading private communication' to his growing list of things he shouldn't have done.

Mom: Fantastic photo! Michael would have loved this :)

Gus's hand stilled on the latch. *Michael?*

Across the hall, the spray of water in the shower stopped. *Bugger.* Gus eyed the critter in the cage. If he was going to do this, he had to get a cracker up him—if he could ignore the guilt burning holes through his stomach.

His father's face flashed before his eyes. It morphed into a weather-beaten, land-roughened, unsmiling … Gus.

He shuddered.

Stuff it. Before he could talk himself out of it, Gus opened the latch on the cage and pulled the animal out. Seconds later, he quietly closed Maya's bedroom door behind him, an empty cage in his hand.

Chapter Eleven

Maya hung her towel over the back of her chair and yawned. What a day. Feeding sheep, dodging lizards and cuddling koalas. She could have done without the legless lizard encounter, but holding Fraser had brought a smile to her face. She'd ask Gus about the kangaroo feeding next, and anything else he thought might be fun to do while she was here. Now that she'd decided to give her stay on the farm a fair shot, she was determined to throw her enthusiasm behind everything he suggested. There was one black mark spoiling this trip that she couldn't do much about—Gus missing his summer school because of her. She'd at least try and take Gus's mind off the fact that he was meant to be elsewhere.

She grabbed her hairbrush off her bedside table and spotted a text from Mum on her phone … *Michael would have loved this :)* An achy warmth spread through her. She swallowed the thickness forming in her throat and reached for the tatty notebook stashed in her bedside drawer. It hadn't been a whole week yet, but one extra entry wouldn't hurt. Just this once. A reward for getting the list started.

She typed a quick goodnight text to her mother, climbed under the bedcovers and flipped through the pages until she found what she was after.

January 16 – Adventures in Antifreeze.

Maya smiled. She'd made an unholy mess on the garage floor that day. She snuggled deeper under the covers, ready to savour every word.

There are several handy uses for antifreeze. As a car engine coolant, to clear ice from your driveway and, according to one craftly old lady, to knock off your family.

The entry was only a page long, but by the end of it her eyes were heavy with the day's events and bittersweet memory. She slipped the notebook into the safety of her bedside drawer. With a click, she switched off the beside lamp and was plunged into sudden darkness. No neighbouring house lights. No overhead streetlights. Other than the stars winking through the window, no lights anywhere.

She could never get used to this freakish black—

Something cold brushed Maya's foot. She jumped up out of bed, scrambled across the room and fumbled for the light switch. *What the heck was that?* She stared at the sheets at the foot of the bed. *Did something just move?* Heart racing, she grabbed the bottom edge of her sheet and flung it away.

And exhaled.

Her belt buckle shone a dull silver near the foot of the bed. It must have slipped under the covers when she unpacked her clothes yesterday. Maya shook her head, a bubble of nervous laughter escaping. *Stupid belt buckle.* With a last steadying breath, she hopped back into bed. This time she was ready for the dark that swallowed the room.

Eyes beginning to close, she felt the flick of something against her cheek. *What now?* She swatted the space near her face—and came in contact with something cold and scaly.

And hissing.

Hissing! What the—

She shot out of the bed so fast the room spun in the absolute darkness. Her foot whacked the edge of the wardrobe. *Argh!* Pain knifed her big toe as she scrambled to find the bedroom door. *Out. Gotta get out.*

Her hands found the cool metal of the door handle. She tore out of the room like the zombie apocalypse had started and hers was the tastiest brain.

'What's going on?' Eyes wide with alarm, Patrick wheeled down the hallway.

'Snake.' Maya pointed into her room with one shaky hand while she rubbed her toe with the other. 'I think there's a snake in my bed.'

Patrick stiffened in his wheelchair, eyes zeroing in on where she rubbed her foot. 'Did it bite you?'

'Did what bite you?' Gus came to stand behind Patrick.

'Maya says there's a snake in her room.'

Gus, too, looked down at her foot.

Maya stopped rubbing it. 'I stubbed my toe,' she explained, 'but no bites, I don't think.' She brushed her hand over her cheek. Surely she would have felt a bite. It must only have flicked her with its tongue. She shuddered. *Eww!*

Mr and Mrs Robertson came rushing down the hallway.

Mrs Robertson wrapped her arm around Maya's shoulders. 'It's probably only a tree python.' *Only* a tree python? There was nothing *only* about any snake, tree python or otherwise. 'They're harmless, I promise.' Mrs Robertson rubbed Maya's arm. It did little to reassure her.

'Let's take a look then.' Mr Robertson stepped into the dark room and flicked on the light. 'In your bed, you said?' Slowly, he edged inside, eyes in the direction of the bed.

Maya craned her neck to keep him in sight but stayed well away from the door—in the safety of the hallway.

'Well, would you look at that.' The man chuckled. *Chuckled! What's so funny about a snake in someone's bed?* 'It's just a Bluey.'

A Bluey? What on earth is a Bluey?

Patrick caught the confused look on her face. 'A blue tongue lizard,' he said.

Sure enough, Mr Robertson emerged out of the room holding a scaly foot-long reptile across one arm. The creature stuck a broad blue tongue out at Maya. *Again, eww!* At least now the name Bluey made sense.

'Lord knows how he found his way into your bed, but he's no snake. Here, have a pat.' Mr Robertson held him out.

Maya jumped back against the wall and concentrated on steadying her breathing. 'Ah, I'm good. Thank you.'

'He's harmless. Promise.' Patrick sent her a reassuring smile and reached across to run his palm over the lizard. On cue, the animal flicked out its broad blue tongue at everyone. 'The tongue is just for show, because look at these things …' He pointed to one of the lizard's short and stubby front legs. 'It's not like they're going to help him run away from anything. The tongue's his only defence against predators.'

Maya crossed her arms. She wasn't sold. 'He hissed at me.' All angry and threatening like a punctured radiator.

Patrick's lips twitched. 'Fine then, the blue tongue *and* the hissing are his only defences.'

Mr Robertson placed the lizard in Patrick's lap. 'Why don't you go give the poor fella a bite to eat to help him get over his shock, then release him out back.'

What about my shock? Not that Maya's stomach could handle a bite of anything right now.

'Come on.' Patrick tipped his head in the direction of the kitchen. 'You can add feeding a Bluey to your *must-do* list.'

'More original than any of the other items,' came Gus's mumble from behind.

Maya sent him an unimpressed glare and followed Patrick into the kitchen. Unfortunately, Gus felt the need to come too. Again, why did Gus have to be the one who looked after her while she was here? Patrick was so much nicer.

Gus fetched a plate of sliced ham from the fridge and dangled a piece out to the lizard. The reptile gobbled it up in two greedy bites. *Suffering from shock, yeah, right.*

'Here, give him a feed.' Gus held the plate out to her.

Maya eyed the ham like it might leap off the plate and bite her.

'It's fine, really.' Patrick edged his wheelchair closer. He had to keep hold of the lizard, who was doing his best to climb out of his lap and onto the plate of meat. 'It won't hurt you. I promise.'

Maya was still wary—the lizard looked like an overfed snake—but Patrick was relaxed, even with the thing wriggling in his lap. Maya gritted her teeth and reached for a piece of ham, her hand only shaking marginally.

She held it out to the animal and—*whoop*—the meat was gone. She looked down at her hand and counted five fingers. *Phew.* The lizard was beady-eyed and scaly, but harmless enough. She swiped another piece of ham off the plate and fed it some more.

'How do you think it got into my room?' she asked, eyes on the Bluey.

Patrick shrugged. 'Don't know. It's not unusual for lizards to wander into a house, especially the little garden skins, but I've never heard of a Bluey crawling into someone's bed before.'

'Maybe you left a window open?' Gus offered across the kitchen where he was putting the ham back in the fridge.

'A Blue Tongue isn't going to climb up into a window,' Patrick said. 'Doesn't matter. No harm done.' The lizard was attempting an escape again, crawling onto the armrest of the wheelchair. 'We better let him out before he loses his cool.'

Maya and Patrick watched from the front veranda as Gus lowered the Bluey onto the mulch under the shrubs lining the front of the house. As soon as the lizard hit the ground, he took off into a pile of leaf litter under one of the bushes. 'He'll be safe from Ralph here. By morning he'll have found himself a nice hidey hole somewhere.'

'Do you think he'll come back and, you know, try to get into the house again?' Maya tried to sound casual about the possibility.

Gus ran his thumb along his jaw, thinking. 'Not likely, but you never know.'

Oh great. She'd have to add sweeping her bed and room for

uninvited bedtime visitors to her evening routine. She was mentally tallying all possible hiding places in her small room, when she caught Patrick shaking his head.

'Quit spooking her, Gus.' He turned to look at her, face open and reassuring for the second time that night. 'In the twenty years I've lived here, this is the first time I've known a lizard to climb into one of our beds. You saw him just now—' he pointed in the direction the Blue Tongue had disappeared, '—they like hiding under shrubs and leafy rubbish, not bed sheets. The whole thing is a bit bizarre, don't you reckon?' He looked across at his brother.

Maya did too.

Slowly, Gus nodded. 'Sure, yeah. Not often you find a Bluey in your bed. More likely a tree snake ends up under your covers.'

Maya's jaw went south. 'Are you serious?' She gripped the veranda railing for balance.

'Not in your bed.' Patrick sent Gus a warning glare.

'But in the house?' *Please don't say yes. Please don't say—*

'Sometimes.' Patrick cringed. 'In the summer we get the odd tree snake in the house.'

Maya sucked in a breath.

'But they're harmless, like the Bluey,' Patrick rushed to explain.

'Yeah, he's right.' Gus leaned against the railing beside her and nodded. 'It's the Eastern Browns you have to worry about.'

Maya made a sound at the back of her throat, a little like she was choking on her own fear.

'Will you stop already!' Somehow Patrick managed to both roll his eyes and glare at Gus at the same time. 'At this rate you'll have Maya packing her bags and tearing out of here before sunrise tomorrow morning.' He wheeled closer and placed a gentle hand on Maya's arm. 'It's really not that bad. He's exaggerating.'

But Gus didn't respond. And Maya was too busy sucking enough air into her lungs so she didn't pass out to wonder why he stayed so quiet.

Chapter Twelve

Gus's stomach tightened when he spotted the plate of ham sitting on the breakfast table. It was a sign the others were already up and had eaten. It also reminded him that revenge wasn't the only thing best served cold. So was guilt, apparently—cured and salted, with a rind much thicker than Gus's skin. Gus did his best to ignore the feeling and went about making his breakfast. If he had to eat the ham, he'd drown it in egg yolk and hide it between toast.

He should have been happy. The Bluey had done its job better than expected. He never dreamed it would wander all the way up to the bed head to hiss Maya out of her skin. Add his strategic hints about Eastern Browns making surprise appearances in houses and he was sure she was close to bailing.

So why did he feel like crap warmed up? Because the whole thing stank of *jerk*, that's why. And Gus wasn't the type who enjoyed being a jerk.

Think of the summer course. Your last chance. Your last bloody chance! Gus ground his teeth and cracked an egg into the frying pan. He had to do this, even if he hated how it made him feel. And he *really* hated how it made him feel, because he couldn't help thinking about how it made Maya feel.

'Morning.'

Speaking of which … Gus looked over his shoulder to find Maya shuffling into the kitchen, the dark smudges under her eyes proof that *Operation Lizard Gate* had worked well into the night. Her eyes also made a lie of the *Little Miss Happy Mechanic* T-shirt she wore. *A Little Miss Tired and Grumpy* tee would have been more on trend this morning.

'Morning.' He tipped his head at the carton of eggs on the counter. 'Want me to fry you some up?' That was the least he could do after what he'd put her through last night.

She yawned but shook her head. 'Do you have any of that Vegemite stuff? I thought I'd knock over another item on my list.'

That bloody list. He shook his head and pulled a jar of Vegemite from the shelf next to him, handing it to her. 'Bread's in the bread box next to the fridge.'

She thanked him, then eyed his cup of coffee like it held the cure to all that ailed her.

Gus pointed to the coffee plunger and tin of fresh grounds on the shelf behind her, then to the kettle. 'I've just boiled it. Should still be hot,' he said, passing her a mug.

She didn't waste any time making her cup of wake-me-up juice. 'So are we heading out to feed the sheep again or are we doing something else today?' she asked, popping two bits of bread in the toaster.

'Something else.'

'What then?'

Gus slid his eggs onto a plate. 'I thought we'd get your hands dirty in a different way today, namely by taking a look at one of our broken quad bikes.' Gus's stomach tightened again—so many types of guilt had his intestines in a bow. He hadn't ridden a quad for years; avoided them whenever he could. A challenge on a farm that used quads on a regular basis.

'What's wrong with it?' Maya asked.

The toast popped. Gus carried it and his eggs to the table.

'Won't start,' he said. 'One of the farm hands thinks it might be the carburettor. He had trouble with bad fuel blocking the line a few weeks back, so that's probably the problem again. Think you can fix that?'

Maya's face pinched, deep grooves digging into her forehead as she spread Vegemite on her toast. 'I've played around with motorbikes but not so much quad bikes. I don't know if it's a good idea for me to fiddle about with—'

'It's not like you can break anything. It's broken already. Come on, give it a go.' Because he really needed her in that shed today.

She took a sip of her coffee, chewed a bit on her bottom lip. 'I guess I could try draining the fuel and cleaning the line ...'

He nodded, relieved. And impressed. For someone who lived on a farm, Gus's knowledge of auto repairs extended to changing a flat tyre.

'Okay, I'll give it a try.' She smiled at him, a sparkle of something like excitement in her eyes.

'Perfect.' And it was perfect—for phase two of his plan. Even if it meant he had to get up close and personal with one of the quad bikes.

Suddenly serious, Maya eyed the toast on her plate, took a deep breath and lifted a piece to her mouth. Gus grabbed her arm before she could take a bite. 'You might want to start with a thinner helping.' He nodded at the tar-thick layer of Vegemite on her toast. 'That stuff tastes like paint stripper at the best of times, but that much in one go will leave you bent over the toilet for the next couple of hours.'

Maya glanced at her toast, then back up at him. 'You don't like Vegemite?'

Gus screwed up his face in answer. She took his advice and scraped the bulk of the black poison off her toast.

He watched her face as she took a bite, waiting for her to gag or spit it out. She didn't. Instead, she chewed, slowly, stretching the moment like it was something to savour even while she blinked at the taste, eyes watering at the yeasty saltiness.

Or something else?

'You don't have to finish,' he said quietly.

She took another bite in reply.

Gus huffed into his coffee. 'It's your list, Maya. You can change it if you like.'

She smiled at him, the sudden cloud in her eyes making him pause mid-sip. 'That's just it. I can't.'

Gus leaned back in his chair and watched her take another determined bite. What was it with her and this list?

When she was finished, Gus grabbed their plates and stacked them in the dishwasher. 'I'll meet you outside in five. Just need to … you know.' He pointed down the hall in the direction of the bathroom. She nodded and turned for the front door.

Gus waited for the slam of the flyscreen, then ducked into his parents' bedroom. The toy box his mother kept handy for when Aunt Cecily visited with the twins sat at the bottom of the wardrobe. He found what he needed under a rusty old Tonka truck.

On his way out, he passed the bathroom. He paused. He didn't need to visit it like he'd told Maya. But maybe he should raid the medicine cabinet for an antacid. He might just need it, the way his guilt was eating him up at what he was about to do. He closed his eyes and held his breath. *But Maya wants this too.* This wasn't just so he could head to Sydney. Her going home early was in both their interests. Even if Maya didn't see it that way at first.

Chapter Thirteen

It was only nine in the morning, but already the sun whispered a warning against the bare skin of Maya's arms and legs. She sat on the veranda stairs and scanned on either side for movement. Nothing. Not even the spindly leaves of the bushes swayed in the breeze. Because there *was* no breeze. There was also no sign of a scaly blue-tongued lizard. She should have been relieved but … *huh*. She was disappointed. The animal had scared her within an inch of a heart attack last night, so she didn't get a chance to have a good look at it. Now, in the daylight, armed with the knowledge that Blueys were harmless, she wouldn't have minded taking a closer peek at him, maybe even brave touching his snake-like skin.

The screen door creaked behind her. 'We're good to go.' Gus paused beside her to put on his weathered Akubra hat. It suited him, drew attention to the angles of his face, his earth-coloured eyes, the shape of his mouth, especially when he smiled at her like he was doing now.

'What?' Gus's smile turned quizzical.

'Just … your hat.' Maya cleared her throat. 'Very practical in this hot weather.'

'Yeah—' he angled his head down and peered at her from under the rim, '—we're nothing if not practical out here.'

Maya looked away before the expression on her face betrayed her earlier thoughts. Gus was hard enough to handle without the added complication of him knowing she found him, well, kind of hot.

They walked the short distance to the shed in silence. Once inside, the familiar smell of dust and engine oil greeted her like it had yesterday. If it weren't for the traces of hay and animal pelt in the air, Maya could almost close her eyes and pretend she was back home in Dad's garage. With Michael.

With a sigh, Maya took a good look around the huge shed. She'd briefly seen the machinery inside yesterday, but she hadn't spotted the quad bikes all lined up in the far corner. Three of them. And one apparently out of action. Despite her reservations, a familiar tingle of excitement crept up and over her scalp. Quad bikes were new territory for her; a new greasy mechanical challenge.

'Which one's the broken one?' Maya ran a gentle hand along the nearest bike's seat—a blue Honda—as though trying to calm a spooked animal. She smiled to herself. Ah, the irony.

When Gus didn't answer, she looked up. He was staring at the deep red bike last in line, lips tight and face paler than the porcelain of a spark plug insulator.

'Gus?'

He startled, took a step backwards and sucked in a deep breath through his nose. 'The yellow one.' He pointed at the bike sitting in the middle.

Maya craned her neck to get a better look at the metal table strewn with what looked like tools near the shed doors. 'Can I use some of those?'

'Sure. Use whatever you need. I'll wheel the bike closer to the workbench.' Gus took a step forward, then faltered. His face pinched, features pulling tight like he'd stepped on something sharp, but there was nothing on the floor.

Maya frowned. *What's going on?* Did he pull a muscle out in the paddock yesterday and was all push-through-the-pain today?

'I can wheel it over to—'

'I've got it,' he said, voice as tight as his features.

Okay then. She left him to it and went to rifle through the tools on the table. A minute later, she'd found what she needed. Gus had managed to wheel the yellow quad bike into the work area, but beads of sweat dotted his forehead. Maya worried the eggs he'd had for breakfast might make a re-appearance.

'Are you okay?'

Gus sucked in a breath, this time through his mouth. He wiped a palm down the side of his face and took a step back. 'I don't think … I'm just gonna get a drink of water.' Another step. 'I'll be right back.' And he was gone.

Should she follow? Make sure he was all right? What if he passed out on the way? Maya blinked at the yawning shed doors. *What to do? What to do?* Five minutes. If he wasn't back in five minutes, she'd go looking for him.

Satisfied, she turned to the yellow quad bike. *Hello there.* Even with a mud-streaked body and dried grass caked on the wheels, the Honda kicked up her pulse like no guy ever had. Although, as battered as this quad bike was, it had nothing on the yellow 1967 Ford Thunderbird Coupe Michael had bought her for her sixteenth birthday. It'd been in a bad way, beat up and cast aside, its insides creaking for oil, love and mechanical attention. But Michael had looked past all that, seen the little car's—and possibly Maya's— potential, and with a focus few people were capable of, had shown Maya how to patch it up.

Maya felt for her wrist, turned the leather band once, twice. Maybe she could help the little quad, too?

With screwdrivers and a quarter-inch ratchet set all at hand, she inspected the bike. She'd have to remove the gas tank to get to the carburettor. Not an easy job and one she hadn't done alone before. She'd just turned off the fuel valve and was loosening the fuel hose clamps when a shadow fell across the shed doors.

Gus.

Except it wasn't.

'Trying to fix Thelma, hey?' Patrick rolled into the shed and came to a stop beside Maya. 'Mind if I hang around?' He wore a similar Akubra to Gus, although his was darker leather and didn't draw Maya's eyes to his features the way Gus's did.

'Don't mind at all.' It'd been a while since she'd got her hands greasy. Might be safer to have someone around in case she screwed up. 'You can give me a hand. Like by giving me that rag and empty ice cream container on the table over there.'

Patrick nodded and reached behind him to the table.

'So, Thelma?' Maya caught the drips from the fuel hose in the rag and raised an eyebrow at Patrick.

'Yeah, Thelma.' A sheepish smile tugged at the corners of his lips. 'When we were younger, Gus and I named all the machinery on the farm.'

Maya quashed a grin. 'So what are the other quads called?'

'The blue quad is Fergus and the red one …' He gripped the armrests of his wheelchair and shifted in his seat. 'Gus named the red one Thumper.'

'Thumper.' Maya's lips twitched. She couldn't picture Gus naming anything after a Disney bunny. She gave the top of the carburettor a twist. The cap came off without any trouble. 'You didn't happen to pass Gus when you came down here, did you?'

Patrick nodded. 'Said he was heading back to the house.'

'Is he all right? He looked a bit off when he left here,' she said, removing the airbox and popping off the carburettor.

'He'll be fine.' Patrick rubbed the heel of his palm along his thigh. 'He's just not a big fan of quads.'

She left the carbie to drain into an old plastic container and twisted to face Patrick. 'To the point where he turns vomit pale when he sees one?' Gus was a farmer's kid. How on earth was he not a fan of quads? Maya didn't know many people under the age of thirty who wouldn't jump at the chance to ride a quad bike, herself included. She held Patrick's gaze.

His eyes ran the length of the yellow bike before coming to rest on Maya. 'Gus and I used to ride the quads all the time. Rounding up sheep, fixing fences, getting from A to B. They were like an extension of our bodies, we rode on the things so often. One time, we were on our way home after moving stock between paddocks when we decided to race the quads home.'

The fuel had drained from the carbie, but Maya was too focused on Patrick's words to check it for gunk. Her gaze brushed the immobile shape of his legs then lifted to his face, silently willing him to go on.

Patrick's expression was that painful mix of defensiveness-meets-regret that only hindsight can bring. 'I was tired, had a late night the day before. I hit a divot, the quad rolled and …' He glanced over at the red quad bike and ran a hand over his eyes as though to erase the memory.

Maya tried to swallow past the lump in her throat but couldn't.

'The helmet saved my head, but the weight of the quad crushed my spine. Gus hasn't been the same around quad bikes since. He's never said it, but he blames himself.' Patrick's mouth flattened into a thin line. Did he blame Gus? His tone gave no indication either way. She wanted to ask him but chose a safer question instead.

'What about you and quad bikes?' Maya looked from Patrick to the yellow quad and back. Patrick's complexion remained tan. No sign that he was about to rush out and puke.

'We're good,' he said, although Maya didn't miss the frustration in his voice.

'But …?'

'I don't have a problem with quad bikes, but everyone else seems to have a problem with me not having a problem with them.'

Maya frowned.

He sighed, took off his hat and rubbed at his hair. 'I want to help run the farm, be useful again. That means getting back on a quad so I can get around, but every time I suggest we get someone out to alter one of our quads so I can use it, I get shut down. By Dad and Mum and Gus ...' He slapped his hat on the armrest of his wheelchair. 'Especially Gus.'

'They're worried about you.' Maya understood only too well.

'Yeah, I get it, but all that worry is stopping me from doing what I was born to do. What I desperately want to do. They're so adamant, Gus especially, but Dad too. Sometimes I think Dad doesn't want me to ... that he doesn't think I'm ...' He dug his thumb and index finger into the corners of his eyes, a habit so like Gus's that for a moment Maya could have mistaken them for twins. When he looked back up, his eyes sparked with determination. 'I *know* I can do this, Maya. I can be useful on the farm. I just need them to see that this ...' he swept a hand over his legs, '... doesn't have to be a barrier. With the right adjustments here and there, I'd be good to go.'

The right adjustments here and there. Maya glanced at the yellow quad bike, at the handles, the brake. 'What kind of modifications would you need?'

Patrick leaned forward. 'I'd need access to the rear brake with my hands. The quads are automatic, so no gear controls, which means the left front brake could be hooked up to the rear foot pad instead. At least that's what the internet tells me,' he said, with a shrug.

Maya angled her head, skimmed the bike, considered her options ... Could she? She'd need to get some materials, maybe other tools. It wasn't exactly straightforward and Patrick would likely not want his parents to know. She wasn't sure how she felt about making the modifications behind their backs, but Patrick *was* an adult and could make his own decisions, so ...

She took a deciding breath. 'I could give it a go.'

Patrick pushed himself up straighter in his wheelchair. 'Seriously?'

Maya caught Patrick's eye and paused. The look on his face, so hopeful, so thankful, it took her by surprise. Then, just as suddenly as it had appeared, a frown wiped it from his features. He shook his head. 'They'll all say no, and even if we get Mum and Dad to agree, there's Gus—' He forked a hand through his hair. 'Good chance he'll pass out at the idea of me riding a quad again. You saw him.' He waved a hand out the shed doors. 'He was eggshell pale when I passed him earlier. I was surprised he even suggested you come out here with him to look at the broken-down quad.'

Maya frowned and picked up one of the screwdrivers to unscrew the carburettor bowl. Maybe Gus thought it was time to challenge his fear? Or maybe Gus was trying to make an effort and help her feel more at home after the lizard incident? She glanced at the shed door. Whatever it was, he still hadn't come back.

She frowned again. 'He said he'd be back in five minutes. It's been way longer than that.'

Popping his hat back on, Patrick nodded. 'I better go check on him,' he said, and expertly manoeuvred his wheelchair around the tools and bike parts on the floor, and out the shed.

Maya turned her attention to removing the idle and throttle jets. They weren't all that dirty. Neither was the main part of the carbie. Not dirty enough to cause any trouble with the ignition, at least. She cleaned them anyway but suspected something else was preventing the bike from starting.

Ten minutes later, the carburettor was back in place but still no sign of Gus or Patrick. Eyes on the shed doors, Maya wiped her hands on the rag. She should have gone herself.

She hadn't picked up on any tension between the two brothers, but … Her fingers tugged at the leather band on her wrist, toyed with the knot dangling where the ends met—she knew all about the pressing weight of guilt.

She turned the key in the ignition and … nothing. Something else was causing the starter problem. Maybe something as simple as the air filter? She wouldn't look at it now, though. She had to go and find Gus.

Chapter Fourteen

Gus stood at the kitchen sink, glass of water in his hand. His breath came easier now, but the inside of his stomach still felt like it was riding a death-loop rollercoaster.

What had he been thinking? He hadn't been near a quad since Condo's paddock party last December. One of the guys had rocked up on a quad and Gus's hands had started shaking like a newly shorn sheep in a cold snap. So bad he'd spilled his drink all over his pants. Being near a quad flicked some internal switch, and all he saw was Pat hitting that divot and flying head over arse and the bike flipping up and over and the thud—*God, that thud*—as the quad landed on top of …

Gus gulped another mouthful of water. Taking Maya to fix Thelma had been a stupid idea. He could easily have planted phase two of his get-rid-of-Maya initiative somewhere else. Although, the way her face had come alive at the possibility of tinkering with a broken-down piece of machinery, her eyes widening with excitement … He'd almost had a moment of insanity, thinking that maybe six weeks with her around wouldn't be all that bad.

Too late. Any moment now, she'd find his little surprise and make a run for her suitcase.

It's what you want.

Yeah, it *was* what he wanted. But the whole thing was starting to resemble the craving for a supersized McDonald's meal—you desperately wanted one, then felt like crap immediately after having it.

'Hey, you feeling alright?'

Gus whipped his head around to find his brother in the doorway. Pat's brow creased at the sight of his face. He must look worse than he thought.

'Just been with Maya in the shed. She said you raced out of there not looking all that crash hot.'

The concern in Pat's voice was a serrated knife to Gus's already haemorrhaging conscience. Here he was, nursing a panic attack after five seconds next to a quad bike, and the very person who *should* never want to see a quad again was asking Gus if he was all right. If he wasn't so busy trying to keep from barfing all over the kitchen floor, he'd be laughing at the irony.

'I'm fine.' Gus drained the last mouthful from his glass and put it in the sink.

Pat slowly rolled his wheelchair into the kitchen. 'Well, you don't look it.'

'I'll be fine. Probably just ate something dodgy.' Gus's gaze slid away from his brother's. Pat's legs might be bung, but there was nothing wrong with the guy's brain. He knew exactly when and why Gus's aversion to quad bikes had started, even though they'd never really discussed what'd happened that day four years ago.

'I'm fine, really.' Gus wrestled his mouth into something he hoped resembled a smile. 'Just needed a drink to settle my stomach.'

Pat nodded but didn't look convinced. For a panicked moment, Gus was sure his brother was finally going to ask him about the bike, about the way seeing it made his hands shake and his skin pale.

Then a scream cut through the awkward silence.

'Maya!' Pat swivelled his wheelchair for the kitchen door.

'I'll go.' Gus darted past his brother.

But halfway down the path, Pat had almost caught up to him.

Crap. Pat coming along was a complication Gus didn't need.

Inside the shed, he found Maya pressed against the wall behind the quad bikes, the whites of her eyes huge with fear.

'You all right?' He knew she would be physically. Emotionally … well, that was another matter.

'A snake, over there.' She pointed an unsteady hand at the spot where she'd been working on the yellow quad.

Gus whipped around and spotted a coil of brown and yellow on the petrol splattered floor.

He sucked in a breath. 'Looks like an Eastern Brown.'

'Did it bite you?' Pat wheeled past Gus and straight for Maya. He put a hand on her arm, gently rubbing the limb up and down in an attempt to sooth her, calm her. Something Gus probably should have done. But he couldn't bring himself to look her in the eye, let alone touch her. She'd smell the betrayal on him. His gut clenched, and this time it had nothing to do with being in close proximity to a quad bike.

'I don't think anything bit me.' Maya gnawed at her bottom lip. 'I rolled the quad bike back here and only saw the snake when I went to walk out of the shed.' Her eyes widened again and she hugged herself. 'It must've been sitting under the bike the whole time I was working on it.'

'And it's still there.' Pat narrowed his eyes and leaned forward to better look at the snake. 'You'd think all our racket would've sent it scrambling.'

Gus ignored the burn of Pat's glare. 'Give me that shovel.' He waved at the garden tools hanging on a wall near them. 'I'll check it out.'

Weapon in hand, he eased forward. He scanned the work table near the door and—*yes!*—he spied a dirty rag on it. If he played this right, he might still get away with this scam. But he had to act fast—'kill' the snake with the shovel and wrap it up in the rag before Pat and Maya came too close to figure out what was going on.

Gus lifted the shovel and, sharp end leading, brought it down on the snake with a theatrical grunt. A bit of side to side grinding with the edge, and the whole thing could have won an Oscar.

'It's dead,' he said, quickly reaching for the rag.

'It's rubber.' Pat's unimpressed voice came from behind Gus before he could cover the evidence.

Shit. Gus briefly closed his eyes. *Think. Think!* The only way out was to act dumb. 'Rubber? Really?'

Pat crossed his arms and leaned back in his wheelchair. 'Rubber. *Really.*' His tone made it clear he wasn't buying any of this award-winning act.

'Which is it then?' Maya asked, cautiously coming towards them. 'Dead or rubber?'

Gus made a show of poking the snake with the shovel, which earned him a snort from his brother. He ignored it. When the rubber snake did nothing more than shake like jelly at his poking, Gus bent to pick it up. 'Well, look at that. It really *is* rubber.' He cringed and turned away, so Maya didn't see. Man, he sounded like a tool.

When he looked back up, Maya's brow could have passed for corrugated iron.

'So what's a rubber snake doing under the quad bike I was fixing?' Her gaze bounced between Gus and Patrick.

Gus couldn't detect any accusation in her voice, only genuine confusion. He eyeballed his brother, sending a silent *SOS*.

Pat pursed his lips. 'That's an excellent question.' He peered at Gus from beneath a raised brow.

Gus worked his jaw. Pat wasn't blowing his cover, but it didn't look like he'd be helping him out either.

Licking his lips, Gus peered at the limp rubber snake in his hand. It looked a bit like he felt right now—out of options. He wiped his other palm, now clammy, down his shorts and scratched his head. 'I have no idea how this got in here. Maybe the last time the twins were visiting ...' Gus trailed off, eyes scanning the shed roof like he might find the answer to his problem in the rafters.

The rafters!

'We used to hang fake snakes from the rafters—' he pointed above his head, '—to stop birds nesting in the shed. This must be one of them.' Gus gave Maya a *problem-solved* nod. Pat rolled his eyes but kept quiet. Gus's shoulders shed some tension.

Then Maya's expression shifted from confused to sceptical. 'If it fell from the rafters, wouldn't it have landed on the bike, not under it?' She crossed her arms.

The action tightened her T-shirt in interesting places, but Gus was sweating too much to appreciate the sight. 'It must have dropped before we came in, and somehow I missed it when I rolled the quad over to the work bench. But that's not surprising since I wasn't feeling the best, so …' Gus shrugged, half in apology, half in a couldn't-be-helped gesture. 'Let's just be glad the thing isn't real.'

Pat gave another snort and Gus had to curb the urge to flip him the bird. Maya's eyes were bouncing between them again, the creases on her brow increasing. This whole thing had turned into a bloody balancing act. One wrong move—most likely by his eye rolling, snorting brother—and his badly constructed lie would come crashing down around him and his rubber snake.

Surprisingly, it was Pat who came to his rescue. 'Come on. Let's get you out of here.' He gestured to Maya. 'I reckon you could use a drink and a sit down after the scare you've just had. And I want to hear whether or not you managed to fix the bike.'

Maya looked like she might fire more questions at Gus, but an encouraging smile from Pat changed her mind. Pat waited until Maya stepped out into the yard, then threw Gus a *you've-got-some-explaining-to-do* glare over his shoulder.

Gus ran a hand over his face. Now there was a conversation he wasn't looking forward to. He chucked the rubber snake on the work bench and rubbed at his stiff neck. What a complete stuff-up. The snake might have spooked her, but he doubted it was enough to send her packing. And now he had Pat to contend with, too. All the while, the Sydney summer school had well and truly started.

Chapter Fifteen

'It's not the carburettor.'

Maya took a sip from the tumbler of water Patrick had given her and pulled out a chair from the kitchen table. She was still buzzing with the wrong kind of energy, her body wound tight—*coiled*—like the stupid rubber snake. The whole thing had rattled her. Not just because it'd nearly caused her first plumbing malfunction since she'd left toddlerhood, but because something was off about Gus's *fallen-from-the-rafters* explanation. His desperate scramble for an explanation, the deliberate way he held her gaze … It didn't sit right.

'I cleaned the carburettor,' she said, 'and the quad still wouldn't start.'

'Any idea what it could be then?' Patrick filled the kettle at the kitchen sink and Maya scratched her temple. The eleven o'clock sun pushed against the glass of the kitchen window like it wanted to set the bowl of apples beneath it on fire, but that didn't stop Patrick from insisting he make Maya a cup of tea.

'My money's on the air filter,' Maya said over the hum of the kettle. 'If that's it, it's a five-minute fix.'

Patrick put teabags into two mugs and smiled across at her. The unsettling buzz in her body eased a little—there was something therapeutic about Patrick's smiles.

A lot like Michael's.

The kettle hissed and Patrick poured boiling water into the mugs. He settled the cups on a tray in his lap and made his way over to the table. 'We can have another look at the quad later if you're up to it.'

When she didn't respond, his face pinched with concern. 'After we check the shed for snakes.'

Maya tried for a smile but couldn't quite get there. 'How often do you find non-rubber snakes in the shed?'

Pat considered her over the rim of his mug. The longer he sipped at his ridiculously hot tea, the harder Maya's leg bounced under the table.

Finally, he lowered his tea. 'Look, I won't lie to you—' he looked directly at her, '—we see a fair few snakes around the farm in summer.'

Maya swallowed and stilled her leg. 'How many is a fair few?'

Pat worked his jaw, pursing his lips. 'Three to five?'

Maya's breath stuttered and Pat's open palm came up to calm her. 'But usually in the paddocks or sheds. It's been years since we found an Eastern Brown in the house and no-one's been bitten by one in the twenty years I've lived here.' His eyes crinkled with concern. He was trying so hard to reassure her. 'Honest, Maya. You're safe. I promise.'

She wanted to believe him, but the past twelve hours had really tested her resolve to stick it out in this reptile-infested patch of the planet. Other than the visit to the animal sanctuary, the trip had been a massive disappointment so far. The Blue Tongue, the rubber snake, an arrogant Farmer Boy—it all reminded her she didn't really want to be here.

The distant sound of Emmy's ringtone tugged her attention down the hallway. 'That's my cell. Mind if I—'

Patrick waved her off. 'Go for it.'

Hot tea untouched, she pushed away from the table. A talk with Emmy was just what she needed. Her friend always helped her get perspective. She dashed out the door and rammed shoulders with Gus.

'Sorry,' he said, even though she'd been the one to bulldoze him. He moved out of her way, gaze brushing hers briefly. For a moment,

Maya wondered if his apology was about more than just having bumped shoulders.

The heat of Gus's eyes left the skin between her shoulders prickling. Something was definitely off, and as soon as she finished her phone call, she'd corner Farmer Boy and demand some answers. Hopefully she'd have figured out which questions to ask by then.

A few minutes later, she'd filled Emmy in on the last few days.

'A lizard with a blue tongue?' Emmy sounded horrified. 'Are you okay? Did it bite you?'

Maya smiled, warmth spreading across her chest at her friend's worry. 'I'm fine. It didn't bite me. What I want to know is how it got into my bed.' She threw a nervous glance at her pillow from her vantage point against the open French doors—one foot in her room, the other on the veranda.

'I guess being out on a farm means you'll encounter an unwelcome reptile or two.'

'In the paddocks, yes, but not in my sheets.' Maya shifted on the wooden floors. Just thinking about the flick of that blue tongue on her cheek made her skin crawl.

'But the snake today was fake?'

'Yes, rubber. Fell from the rafters, apparently.'

'You don't sound convinced.'

Maya leaned forward and ran a fingernail along a gap between the floorboards. 'Hanging rubber snakes from the rafters to stop birds from nesting in the shed I can sort of believe, but one falling in exactly the spot where I was fixing the bike and Gus not noticing …' She clucked her tongue against the roof of her mouth. 'Yeah, I'm not convinced.'

'So, what are you saying?'

What was she saying? She wasn't sure. Yes, the snake had been brown and the floor dirty, but the rubber toy would have been hard to miss when Gus wheeled the quad bike closer to the work bench. He must have been in a real state after coming in contact with the bike, because if he hadn't been, that meant he knew the snake was there when he left the shed. Which meant he knew there'd be a good chance she'd find it. *Hmm ...* Maya tapped a thumb against her thigh.

'So you know how Patrick's in a wheelchair? He told me how he got there.' Maya recapped Patrick's story to Emmy.

'What an awful thing to happen,' Emmy whispered.

'Yeah. Patrick's life's been upended and Gus still can't go near a quad bike without freaking out.'

'Must have been hard for him to let you tinker with the bike when he can't stand the sight of the things.'

'Oh, it was.' So why do it? Why put himself in that situation when Patrick could easily have taken her instead?

Her thumb resumed a rhythm on her thigh, faster this time. 'Something about the whole snake thing is off, Em.' The more Maya thought about it, the more convinced she was.

'You don't actually think ...' Her friend's voice lowered with disbelief. 'Are you saying what I think you're saying?'

'I'm not saying he planted the rubber snake, but at the very least he knew it was under the quad.'

'But that would mean he wanted you to find it.'

'Exactly.'

'After the Blue Tongue bed partner you had last night?'

'Especially after the Blue Tongue in my bed last night.'

Emmy sucked in her breath. 'You really believe he'd do something like that?'

Maya's mouth flattened. 'I hope I'm wrong.'

'And if you're right? If he knew about the snake, maybe even planted it, what then?'

Good question; one Maya didn't have an answer to. If it was just a joke—even one in as poor taste as this—she might be able to forgive Farmer Boy. But if it was something else ... Maya didn't know what she'd do.

Yet.

As soon as she hung up from Emmy, Maya went in search of Gus. She expected to find him with his brother, but the kitchen was empty. Gus had been there—a half-full glass of water that wasn't hers stood next to Patrick's tea mug on the table.

Maybe back in his room?

Maya knocked on Gus's door. It creaked open to stand ajar.

'Gus? Hello?'

No answer.

Not in his room. Not in the kitchen, and she didn't see anyone in the living room when she passed it on her way down the hallway. Maybe he was in the bathroom?

Fine. She'd wait.

She leaned against the wall opposite his room. From this angle, she could see through the partly open door. His room looked about the size of hers. Nothing flash. Similar wooden bed to hers, a bigger desk than the one in her room, most of which was taken up with a large desktop, a stationery caddy and a *Jurassic Park* mug sitting on one corner.

Maya craned her neck to get a better look at it. She snorted—the caption read *Tea Rex*.

She went to straighten up when something metallic under the desk caught her eye. She pushed away from the wall and walked over to the bedroom door. A cage. About the size of a microwave. Empty. Too small to fit a dog and she couldn't imagine it would be any use with a sheep. Maya curled that ever-annoying strand of hair around her finger and shoved it behind her ear.

Curiosity talked her into sticking her head through the gap in the door. Closer, she could read the faint writing on the small placard near the latch: *Daranco WIRES Sanctuary*.

Weird. She didn't remember Gus bringing anything back after their visit yesterday. Condo's words scratched at her memory… *there's a small cage behind the front counter for you. It's got the blue—*

Maya's eyes narrowed on the cage, her brain ticking over. The sanctuary, the koala, Gus ducking out to check on the dog. She stiffened, cold steel pouring down her spine. *He wouldn't! Would he?* Because if he did, then this was way worse than just a stupid rubber snake prank.

An agitated voice floated into Gus's room in snatches through an open window.

'… were you even thinking? … could have hurt herself … idiotic prank!' *Patrick*. Out the back on the wrap-around veranda.

Maya debated for a couple of seconds then pushed the door open a little wider and, making sure she couldn't be seen, leaned in.

'She was fine.' *Gus*. She could see his silhouette near the window.

She heard Patrick scoff. 'After the Blue Tongue in her bed last night, she was scared out of her wits.' A pause. 'But that's exactly how you wanted it, right?'

Silence. Maya held her breath.

'What's your end game?' Patrick asked.

Yes, Gus, what is your end game?

She crossed her arms and tracked his shape as, head down, shoulders hunched, he paced the veranda near his window. 'I had other plans for the summer.'

'You're trying to scare her off the farm so you can go surfing with your mates?' Patrick sounded disgusted, and rightly so.

'It was never about the stupid surfing. I'm booked into a—' Gus's head snapped up and his pacing stopped.

Patrick came into view in the bottom left corner of the window. 'Booked into a what?'

Gus was keeping the course a secret from his brother? *Interesting.*

'It doesn't matter,' Gus said. 'She doesn't want to be here. You should have heard her—she called the place a Hicksville backwater.' Maya cringed. He'd heard that? 'I was just helping her make the choice to go home that little bit easier.'

There it was. She glanced at the cage. He'd planted the Blue Tongue and the rubber snake. Gus was trying to scare her off the farm. He wanted her gone.

She slumped against the door frame, inexplicably deflated by the revelation. Yes, she'd badmouthed his hometown and yes, she hadn't exactly jumped up and down with excitement at being on a sheep farm. But a lizard in her bed and a snake to scare her stiff?

Sneaky. Devious. Bordering on nasty.

But two could play at this game.

Chapter Sixteen

As much as Gus dreamt of a life that didn't include sheep, today he envied the stupid creatures their uncomplicated existence. Right now, he would trade places with one of them at the drop of his Akubra. They jostled for prime position near the trough, their brains filled only with thoughts of how fast they could get the feed into their bellies, while Gus couldn't get the look of disappointment on Pat's face out of his head.

He should have told Pat about the summer school. Pat was well aware that sheep weren't Gus's passion, but Gus had never confided his dream of studying computer animation to his brother. Partly in fear that Pat'd let it slip to their parents, but also because he didn't want Pat to think he'd abandon his obligation to the farm.

Pat loved this place and always thought he'd be the one to take over from their father. The accident changed all that, and now neither of them could follow their dreams. Which brought him back to the summer school and his desperation to at least be able to attend some of it.

With a final glance at the ewes, heads down, stuffing their gobs, he climbed into his ute. He didn't bring Maya along today. He couldn't afford her asking him any curly rubber-snake-related questions. Besides, doing the feed by himself was a punishment of sorts.

So he drove into the bottom paddock and helped his parents select weaners to sell off at market, then cleaned out the chook pen and, to round it all off, climbed on the homestead's roof to clear leaf litter from the valleys and gutters. To punish himself further and give himself time to think.

He didn't know if he could keep going with his plan to scare Maya off the farm. Even if she ended up believing his snake-falling-from-the-rafters story, he wasn't sure he had it in him to put her through any more grief. All this sneaking around and lying was exhausting.

From the roof, he spotted Maya and Pat heading back to the machinery shed around afternoon-tea time. She was braver than him, heading back in there. Pat must have reassured her it was snake-free— which Gus should be grateful for. Even in the short time he'd spent with Maya, he could see the shed was a place she felt comfortable in.

Until she'd come across the snake.

Gus crouched in one of the valleys, placed his hands flat on the roof tiles, and closed his eyes. How the hell did he get here? Not just up on a roof, too chicken to face his brother and Maya, but down a path where he'd turned into a liar and downright unlikable human being?

He rubbed a hand across his sweat-streaked face and stood, scanning the farm and the paddocks dotted with tiny clouds of sheep. His family's land stretched as far as the naked eye could see. Maybe it was time to let go of what he wished his life would be and accept it for what it was. And he could start by apologising to Maya.

Tomorrow. He'd start with a clean slate tomorrow. He couldn't face what he deserved tonight.

By the time he finally stumbled into the house, muscles sore and hair full of leaf litter, it was almost seven. He was starving, but he'd deliberately missed dinner, so he didn't have to sit opposite Pat's disapproving frown and Maya's suspicious gaze.

The smell of freshly baked lasagne teased him from the kitchen. Hopefully there was some left over. The plan was to grab a plate after a quick shower, then he'd lock himself in his room and work on his latest project—an architectural walk-through animation featuring a medieval castle.

Tomorrow. Tomorrow he'd apologise.

On his way to the bathroom, voices drifted out from the lounge, over the opening theme of *The Farmer Wants a Wife*. Gus shook his head. His mother had a Masters in Educational Psychology—she was one of the most intelligent people he knew—yet here she was, taken in by this beyond stupid reality TV show. And by the sounds of it, she'd roped Pat and Maya into watching it with her.

His family and Maya were still engrossed in the reality TV drivel when he came out of the bathroom a quarter of an hour later. *Good.* It meant he could slink safely into his room unnoticed, which was fortunate, since he'd forgotten to bring clean underwear and had to make the dash across the hallway wrapped in a towel.

Gus shut the door behind him and leant back against it. Man, he was tired. And hungry. And his face stung. A glance in the wardrobe mirror confirmed the shower had washed away the day's dirt and exposed newly acquired sunburn. He pressed at the dark pink stain on his cheekbone. The white pressure point faded to an even angrier pink. He sighed. Mum would tear verbal strips off him when she saw this.

Clearly, Gus had left his sun sense behind along with his sense of decency.

Another sigh. *Get a grip.* Maybe he'd give the medieval castle project a miss tonight and just crawl into bed after he'd had something to eat.

He pulled open one of the dresser drawers and rifled inside for clean pyjamas, while scanning the top of the dresser for the tube of Aloe Vera cream he'd pilfered from Ruth a few weeks ago.

Bingo! There it was, hiding behind his can of deodorant. He reached for it at the same time as he pulled out a pair of boxers from the drawer. That's when he felt something scurrying up his arm, across his chest and—

'What the—'

He jumped back from the dresser, slapping at his torso. In the wardrobe mirror, he caught sight of eight spindly hairy legs scampering over his shoulder and onto his back.

'Ah! AH!' A huntsman! *Get it off!* Gus twisted, turned, knocked his hip into the dresser, nearly dropped his towel. *Get it off! Get it off!* But he couldn't. It shot up his back and into his hair. 'Off! Get off!' He swatted at his head, desperate to dislodge the critter while at the same time trying not to get creeped out at having to touch the thing.

He flicked the huntsman off his head at the same time as the door swung open.

'What? What is it?' His mother looked him up and down with concern.

'Watch out!' He pointed at the floor where the spider had landed, but the stupid thing took off and—*no! Not there!* Gus swallowed a curse as the palm-sized terror shot into the shadows under his bed. *Well, there goes any chance of sleep tonight.*

His mother huffed, more a sound of relief than annoyance. 'It's only a huntsman.'

Hands finding his hips, Gus worked his jaw. 'Thanks, Mum. I know what it is. How about helping me get it out of my room instead of stating the obvious.' Because as long as it roamed around in here, he wasn't closing his eyes tonight.

His mother rolled hers and sunk to her knees to peek under his bed.

'Want us to get the insect spray?' Maya's voice came from his bedroom door. Her face was a picture of innocence, but her voice said, *Welcome to Mocksville.* Beside her, Pat didn't even bother hiding his amusement.

Gus wanted to swipe the stupid smirk off his brother's face but then realised what his brother—and Maya—were seeing: his mother on her hands and knees checking under Gus's bed for spiders, while he stood there all flustered in nothing but a bath towel.

He cringed. What was he, a toddler asking his mummy to check under the bed for the bogeyman? *For sheep's sake!*

'Mum, please, get up.' He reached down to take hold of his mother's elbow and almost lost his towel. *Crap.* He fumbled but managed to grab hold of the wet cotton before he flashed his bits at everyone in the room. 'I'll sort it. Please, Mum, get up.' The way he tugged on her arm, he didn't give her a chance to argue.

She pushed off her knees and straightened. 'Honestly, the way you carried on I thought you were being murdered in here.'

Gus's face flared under the already warm sting of his sunburn. 'The critter freaked me out.' He stopped fussing with the towel and pointed to his dresser. 'The damn thing was in my underwear drawer!'

His mother's eyes widened. 'How on earth did it get into your underwear drawer?' She frowned and stepped closer. 'Are you sunburnt?'

Gus ignored her second question and focused on the first. He must have left the dresser open and the stupid spider crawled insi—*Hold on a minute.* He glanced at his underwear drawer, the contents neatly tucked inside. He wasn't in the habit of leaving it, or the wardrobe, or anything for that matter, open. He distinctly remembered it had been closed. Tightly shut. How then did a spider get into a *closed* drawer?

Hands finding his hips again, he straightened and narrowed his eyes on the two faces in the doorway. Pat shrugged, but it was Maya's brow, quirking ever so slowly, that grabbed his attention.

She pursed her lips, considering him. 'Maybe you left a window open?'

His words. From last night. About the Blue Tongue.

Gus's mouth popped open. His eyes found the open drawer, swung to the shadows under his bed, then back to Maya. *How on earth …?*

Pat's lips twitched and that's when Gus knew. He knew! The two of them hadn't just been fixing the quad in the shed that afternoon—

they'd scoured the dark, webbed corners for huntsmen. The dirty rotten mongrels!

Gus flattened his lips as irritation rumbled in his stomach. Or maybe that was hunger since he still hadn't eaten. Either way, he wasn't impressed.

His mother patted his arm on her way out the door. 'There's always Ruth's room if you're not comfortable sleeping here tonight.'

That's when Pat lost it. He swivelled his wheelchair around to follow their mother, but the traitor didn't do it fast enough to hide his shoulders shaking with silent laughter.

Maya remained in his doorway. Leaning against it, actually, arms crossed and a look in her eyes he couldn't get a read on.

He leaned against his dresser and crossed his arms, mirroring her. 'I didn't leave a window open. Like I didn't leave any of these drawers here open,' he said, tipping his head at the one containing his underwear. 'Which makes me wonder how a huntsman managed to get into my boxers.' His fingers drummed on his bicep, drawing Maya's eyes to his arm, then down across his torso, to the towel wrapped around his waist.

'I really can't say, but speaking of boxers—' her cheeks darkened with colour, but she looked him straight in the eyes, '—maybe you should put some on?'

Gus shifted, suddenly hyper aware of the fact that he was one wardrobe malfunction away from standing butt naked in front of his house guest.

He grabbed hold of the towel, just in case. 'Maybe, if I had some privacy, I'd do exactly that, so if you don't mind …' He waved a hand over her head, motioning for her to get going and follow the others down the hallway.

But Maya didn't move. If anything, she gave him another once over, the sweep of her eyes sure and bold this time. Mind you, this wasn't the kind of look he was used to getting whenever he happened to find himself shirtless around a girl. It held too much challenge and not enough … appreciation. He frowned—that annoyed him more than it should have, dammit.

'Is there something else you want?' he snapped.

Maya's eyes flared. 'Actually, there is. I've ticked the koala and Vegemite off my list and your mom suggested we do the kangaroo feeding next. Any chance you'd be up for that tomorrow?'

Whatever answer Gus'd been expecting, it wasn't this. 'You want to keep going with your list?'

Maya's head bobbed back in surprise. 'Yes. Why wouldn't I?'

Gus blinked, opened his mouth, closed it again. 'I just thought …'

'Thought what?' Maya cocked her head, dark brown eyes flashing like midnight sky before an electrical thunderstorm. 'It's going to take a lot more than lizards and snakes to scare me away.'

Gus froze, eyes locked on Maya's. She was onto him. Not only that, she'd somehow managed to catch and hide a huntsman in the one place it'd freak him out the most.

It was downright devious.

It was conniving as hell.

It was bloody ingenious and he couldn't help but admire her for her tenacity. Even if she wasn't freaked out by spiders, a fist-sized huntsman was the stuff of nightmares. He'd rather stick his hand up a sheep's privates than willingly go on the hunt for an eight-legged hairy demon.

Suddenly, the guilt that'd plagued him since he'd slipped the Bluey under her sheets lifted a fraction. His lizard and snake antics couldn't have caused her any serious grief if she had the nerve to go catching huntsmen.

And now she wanted to go kangaroo feeding? Fine then.

He nodded, allowed a smile to slowly spread across his face. 'Sure. Kangaroo feeding tomorrow it is.'

Chapter Seventeen

Maya had always been a sound sleeper. One of those out-cold-within-minutes-of-hitting-the-pillow types, even with a racket going on around her. Emmy used to joke that Maya could sleep through the Fourth of July fireworks, and openly envied her friend this ability.

But sleep never again came as easily after Michael had gone.

Now, more often than not, when she closed her eyes her mind opened a Pandora's box of pictures. Michael showing her how to change the brake fluid in an SUV for the first time. Michael explaining the probability of a *MacGyver* hack they'd seen in an episode. Michael putting the keys to Big Bird into her hands.

Michael fighting for breath, panicked eyes losing focus until they stared, unseeing, into a sky so blue it still hurt to think about it.

Maya couldn't remember the last time her head had hit the pillow and she didn't have to fight the scooped-out, hollow feeling the image of her unmoving brother in her arms brought about.

Until last night.

For the first time in over a year, she'd closed her bedroom door, climbed under her covers, and stupid-grinned into the darkness like a clown high on laughing gas—thanks to an image of Gus, all blustery and flustered, pointing an accusing finger at his underwear drawer.

She'd been sceptical when Patrick told her the huge spiders were harmless, but as soon as Patrick revealed Gus hated the things she'd put a lock and bolt on her own mild aversion to the creatures. Ah, the taste of revenge, made that much sweeter by the fact that Gus had been caught with his pants down—*literally.* And Maya had to admit, the guy wasn't exactly an eyesore without his shirt on. Which likely explained why she dreamt of Gus, hands on shirtless hips, as she lay there in the early hours of the morning.

She'd have happily kept on dreaming, but someone pounding on her bedroom door jerked her out of her haze.

'Wakey wakey! Rise and shine,' Gus's voice came through her door.

Wakey wakey? Who even said that? Screwed up vocab aside, the guy sounded way too chirpy for someone who should have spent the night on high alert for eight-legged bed partners.

Maya felt for her phone on the bedside table, peered at the screen and groaned. Half past four. *Is he insane?*

'Maya! You awake in there?'

'Yeah,' she croaked. Half of Barangaroo Creek was awake after his almighty door banging. 'Give me a sec.' She swung unwilling legs onto the floor and felt her way to the bedroom door in the pre-dawn gloom. Rubbing sleep from her eyes, she turned the handle.

'Morning!' Gus's enthusiastic grin was too much to bear this early in the day. It was also not to be trusted, considering the dark smudges under his eyes and bird's nest hair were all evidence of a restless night. By all rights, the guy should be tired and grumpy, not this Mary Poppins ready to break into song.

'What do you want?' A little rude, yes, but Maya's manners were more than a touch rusty before caffeine.

'It's not what I want, but what *you* want,' Gus said, leaning an arm against her door jamb, all casual and relaxed like he was used to getting up at four every day. Well, he probably was, since this was a working farm and sheep had to be fed. All fine and good for Farmer Boy here, but Maya preferred her day buttered on the later side of seven, thank you very much.

Wait, what *she* wanted? She scrunched her nose and scratched her mop of Kamikaze curls. The only thing she wanted right now was to climb back into her bed, close her eyes and maybe conjure a shirtless Gus in her mind's eye. She liked him better flustered and wrapped in a towel than this in-control, fully-dressed, four am version.

Her eyes suddenly widened and travelled the length of him, from his not entirely unimpressive bicep peeking out from under the cuff of his T-shirt, to the teaser of tanned skin exposed between T-shirt hem and shorts. Her gaze snapped back up to his face.

What I want? Is he coming on to me?

His brows rose as though he'd heard her thought. 'Kangaroo feeding, remember?'

She blinked, possibly in relief, but more likely in disbelief. 'What, like now? Are they even up yet?'

Gus's top lip disappeared under his bottom one and suddenly he found the floor near his feet incredibly interesting. Was he laughing at her?

'They come out at dawn,' he said.

Which wasn't for another hour. 'So why on earth did you wake me this earl—'

He straightened and lifted a hand to cut her off. 'You want to hand feed them? Then you've got to offer them something more enticing than dry grass.'

Maya frowned. 'Like what?'

Gus slipped his hands into his back pockets and nodded. 'Sea spray grevillea. They love the stuff.'

Sea spray grevillea? She'd never heard of the plant. But then she hadn't heard of Blue Tongue lizards before this trip either.

Maya frowned. 'So where exactly do we find this … grevillea?'

Gus pointed at the bedroom window behind her. 'The Tinkler's farm next door. Mrs Tinkler has some fenced off growing in her back garden. She's very precious about it, so we'll have to *borrow* some without her knowing.'

Maya wound a strand of frizzy hair around her finger and slipped it behind her ear. She didn't like the idea of stealing somebody else's plants. 'There's nothing else we can feed them?'

'Relax.' Gus grinned like bush-napping was something he did on a regular basis. 'She won't even know we were there. *If* we get in and out before sunrise. So better hurry and get dressed.' His eyes dropped briefly to her tank and shorts pyjama combo. Suddenly the air between them contracted.

Maya tugged at the hem of her tank and inched back from the door slightly. 'Give me five minutes,' she mumbled. Enough time to pull on some clothes, wrestle her hair into submission, and splash some water on her face to help her wake up fully.

And douse whatever it was that'd just sparked between her and Gus.

Chapter Eighteen

The sun flirted with the idea of rising, but it would be another three quarters of an hour before it came through with the goods. Gus, however, was surprisingly awake for someone who'd barely slept the night before. He'd stayed in his room. Pride—and the fear of looking like a wussy little toddler—drove him to risk another close encounter of the huntsman kind. Which meant he lay awake all night with plenty of time on his hands to make sure this morning's kangaroo feeding would be one Maya never forgot. He grinned. Being up before sunrise had never been so worth it.

True to her word, Maya showed on the front veranda at quarter to five. 'All right, I'm good to go,' she said, sweeping her dark shoulder length hair into a quick ponytail. 'Are we taking the pickup?'

'The ute,' Gus corrected, starting down the veranda stairs. 'Yes,' he said, *and no*. But she didn't need to know that yet.

Five minutes later, the Tinkler's homestead rose on the horizon. Gus pulled the ute over to the side of the dirt road and killed the engine. Without the headlights, the road and surrounding fields plunged into darkness.

Maya shifted in the passenger seat. His sight had adjusted enough for him to see the whites of her eyes questioning him. 'Why are we stopping?' she whispered. 'We're nowhere near the gate.'

'We don't want to announce our arrival, remember?' He pulled on the handbrake and opened his door. 'We're walking the rest of the way.'

'Walking. Right.' Maya didn't sound overly impressed but followed him out into the pre-dawn darkness anyway. *So trusting.* A pang of guilt pulled at his chest. But the memory of a huntsman crawling all over his head helped get rid of the tightness quick smart.

They crept towards the house, the uneven dirt road combined with the semi-darkness making it slow going. As much as Gus didn't enjoy early mornings, he could see their appeal. The quiet, the cool stillness, the smell of dry dirt, dry grass and dry livestock hide. A strange anticipation hung in the air before the day took its first breath.

Soon, the fence at the side of the property loomed before them. Gus dug around in his back pocket and handed Maya a calico bag and a small pair of clippers. 'Here. You'll need these once we're over the fence.'

She eyed the chest-height wood palings and frowned. 'How are we meant to get over exactly?'

Gus crouched against the fence. 'I'll give you a boost up.'

Maya glanced at his hands, fingers threaded and ready to hoist her up, and screwed up her nose. Gus swallowed his grin. As he'd suspected, she wasn't keen on this idea. She didn't complain though, just sucked in a big breath and placed her foot into his hold.

'On three,' he said and heaved her onto the fence.

She wobbled about a bit and let out a small yelp, but managed to pull herself up high enough to get a leg over. Gus followed, pulling himself up to find a safe sitting position beside her. He had to make sure the palings didn't skewer anything important.

'Anything I need to know before I jump down on the other side?' she asked.

'Not really.'

She nodded and jumped. Then let out a yelp when she landed.

'Except maybe the spindly grass along the fence,' Gus said,

injecting a wince into his voice. 'The tips of that stuff are really sticky and a real pain if it gets onto your clothes or hair.'

Maya glared up at him from where she'd landed smack in the middle of the waist long grass. 'Thanks for the warning,' she said, hands reaching for her hair.

'Sorry.' Gus carefully lowered himself to the ground, avoiding the grass. He brushed at the front of his shorts and looked around as though to find his bearings. Not because he needed to find the grevillea bush—he knew exactly where that was—he just had a hard time keeping a straight face and needed an excuse to look anywhere but at Maya.

'Come on. It's this way.' He started towards the house. She followed, steps careful and close on his heels. As soon as they'd cleared the side of the house, Maya grabbed the back of his T-shirt in a death grip.

'Doghouse!' She pointed across the yard, her voice was a panicked whisper.

'Empty.' He turned to face her, making sure she saw the truth in his eyes. 'The poor mutt was older than religion and finally barked his last a few weeks ago.'

Maya's sceptical gaze bounced between him and the doghouse.

'I promise.'

She sized him up for another second, then nodded.

They crept on, slowly, but she kept a chokehold on his T-shirt all the way to the far end of the house, where the sea spray grevillea sprawled chest-high along a narrow path between a garden pond and the homestead's back wall.

Gus pulled out his own pair of clippers and a second calico bag. 'It's slim pickings this time of year cause it's stopped blooming, but feel around for the fresher flowers and cut the branch about halfway down,' he whispered.

They worked away at the grevillea in silence, the only sounds the snip of the clippers and rustle of the grevillea branches until—

'Ow!' Maya jerked her hand from the bush. 'What is it with the spikey plants around here?'

'Spikey?' Gus pulled a face. 'Sea spray grevillea is definitely not spikey.' The blue-grey foliage was downright soft.

Maya rubbed her hand. 'The one with the yellow flowers is.'

Yellow flowers? Gus took a closer look at the plant in front of Maya. Sure enough, branches of a bush with bulbous yellow flowers poked out between the red grevillea heads. *Prickly-leaved Paperbark maybe?*

'Then don't touch the one with the yellow flowers.' he said, turning back to his snipping.

Maya huffed. 'Are you always so full of wisdom first thing in the morning?' she asked, braving the plant again.

'Not usually—' Gus dropped a grevillea head into his bag. 'Guess you lucked in.'

Maya snipped a flower head a bit too viciously. 'You know, you're just like these plants—' she hissed at him, '—nice to look at but a pain up close.'

Gus's clippers froze. Brows rising, he turned Maya's way. 'You think I'm nice to look at?'

Maya gaped at him. '*That's* what you take away from that comment?' She shook her head and attacked the grevillea with her clippers again.

'Go easy on that plant or it'll—'

'Ow!' Maya jerked back and rubbed her elbow.

'—fight back.' Gus swallowed his grin. Prickly-leaved Paperbarks weren't dangerous but could cause a decent scratch or two. 'Come on, I'll swap with you,' he whispered, edging over her way. 'Wouldn't want you to get all cut up or get a rash or something.'

'Rash?' Maya's eyes widened. She took a sudden step back from the shrub. 'What kind of plant is thi— Ahh!'

Arms flailing, calico bag flapping about, she lost her centre of gravity and tipped backwards—smack bang in Mrs Tinkler's fishpond.

There was no way Gus could hide his grin. Once Maya surfaced, she was too busy wiping frog larvae off her face to see it. He allowed himself a couple of seconds to enjoy the sight, then reached a hand down to help her.

'You alright?' Lacing his voice with genuine-sounding concern was hard work. He must have done a lousy job if Maya's filthy glare was anything to go by.

She slapped a sudden hold on his arm, the whites of her eyes flaring wide, and for a second he was sure she'd pull him into the water. Part of him didn't mind the idea; she was kinda cute all fired up and gutsy, even covered in frog goo.

She almost got her chance—a sharp bark from across the yard had him half tripping into the water.

Maya jolted for the edge of the pond. 'You said there was no dog!'

Gus helped her scramble out of the water. 'I didn't know, I swear!' If he'd known he never would have brought her here.

The barking was getting louder and closer.

'This way.' Gus pulled her onto a side path and they bolted. The dog's bark followed. Gus risked a glance over his shoulder. The Tinkler's new Blue Heeler was no more than a pup, but he couldn't guarantee it wouldn't nip them when it caught up, especially since they'd given it a reason to chase them by running.

Punishing their legs with their pace, they rounded to the front of the house, then looped back to the side where they'd originally jumped the fence, the Blue Heeler close on their heels. Maya looked ready to make a leap for the fence, but Gus grabbed her by her sopping T-shirt and pulled her a couple of metres down along the fence to a gate. They slid through and slammed it shut behind them with a rattle, leaving the cattle dog barking and scratching at the wood on the other side.

Gus crouched on the dirt road, lungs burning as they grabbed at the night air for breath. He looked up to check on Maya. Big mistake. Bent forward, hands gripping her thighs, she glared at him from beneath clumps of wet hair.

'There's a gate?' she hissed between gulps of air. 'You made me jump the fence when there was a perfectly good gate?'

'I didn't think it'd be open.'

Her nostrils flared. 'What, like you didn't think there was a dog either?'

He winced. 'They must have bought a new one.' He really hadn't known about the dog, but Maya's stab-like expression made it clear she wasn't buying anything that came out of his mouth at the moment.

'We better get moving before the Tinklers come to investigate all that barking.'

She threw him one more dirty look but followed him silently back to the ute.

'Seriously though, you alright?' he asked when they'd climbed into the car. As funny as seeing her all sopping wet and flustered was, the dog had never been part of the prank.

'I can't move without squishing pond water all over my seat and I might need medication to bring my heart rate down to normal, but other than that, yeah—' Maya slammed the passenger side door, '—I'm okay.'

Gus kept quiet. Seventeen years of living in the same house as his sister meant he knew there was nothing he could say right now to defuse this situation. He started the car instead and did a quick U-turn.

A minute or so down the road, he risked a sideways peek at Maya. Dawn filtered through the windscreen, giving him a good view of what he assumed had once been a bright red T-shirt. On impulse, Gus lifted a hand to pick the frog eggs off Maya's shirt, but the stiff-as-a-cattle-prod way she sat in her seat, eyes forward and hands gripping the limp calico bag with her drowned grevillea cuttings … *Yeah, nah.* Might be better to give it a miss.

Who knew what she was plotting in that fuming head of hers?

It'd be hard for her to outdo the huntsman stunt, but if that arachnid horror story had been her creative thinking, then he could only imagine what she came up with in retaliation for today. Another animal hidden somewhere in his room? Nah, too predictable. Maya's *must-do* list might be clichéd, but the girl herself definitely wasn't. Something with machinery maybe? Yeah, that was her comfort zone, so highly likely.

A smile stole across Gus's face before he wrangled it back into submission. He risked another glance Maya's way. Despite himself, he was looking forward to seeing what she came up with next.

A fact that surprised him as much as the girl herself was starting to.

Chapter Nineteen

If someone had told Maya a week ago that she'd be sitting in a pick-up on her way back to a sheep farm in country Australia, watching the sun claw its way over the horizon, while she tried to ignore her pants squelching every time she shifted in her seat, she'd have collapsed in a fit of laughter. But here she was, smelling like a fishpond and trying to dislodge wet underwear without drawing attention to herself.

She hated this place.

She looked over at Gus, took note of the line of his lips, the corners not exactly turned up but also not exactly frowning with worry for her either. *Didn't think there was an open gate, or a spindly bush, or a dog.* Okay, so he could be telling the truth about the dog, but the rest … *not buying it!* This whole grevillea-napping scenario reeked of a set-up. Her grip tightened on the soggy calico bag in her lap. She looked inside. The flowers were crushed and limp and any self-respecting kangaroo would likely turn up its nose at them. That's if they even liked eating the things in the first place.

Maya's head snapped up. She narrowed her eyes at Gus. She wouldn't put it past him to make something like that up just to get back at her.

She pulled a soggy bloom out of her bag and waved it in Gus's direction. 'Do kangaroos really eat these? And I want a no-bullshit answer.'

'You're questioning my kangaroo diet knowledge? I'm offended.'

'I'm questioning your honesty.'

Gus's mouth dropped open and his brows nearly hit the car roof. 'Why would I lie about something like that?'

Maya crossed her arms over her damp T-shirt. 'You tell me,' she said through clenched teeth.

Gus shot her a quick glance, then faced forward, thumb tapping away at the steering wheel. 'No bullshit, the roos really dig sea spray grevillea. But don't take my word for it,' he said, turning onto the Barangaroo Creek Estate drive and pulling the ute to a stop at the side of the house. 'See for yourself.' He pointed out the windscreen. The paddock past the back garden was dotted with kangaroo silhouettes.

'There's no guarantee they'll come closer,' he said, hopping out of the ute. 'But there's not a lot of grass out there, so they're more likely to come check out what we've got on offer.'

Still sceptical, Maya scrunched her nose but followed Gus into the paddock, mangled grevillea flowers in hand. Slowly, they crept nearer, Maya taking her lead from Gus. The kangaroos had spotted them but didn't make any moves to scatter. Tension pulled at Maya's shoulders the closer they came to the animals. They weren't small— some of them towered over her by a couple of feet when standing upright—and the claws on their paws would have set off anyone's nervous eye twitch.

'Have you ever fed them by hand before?' Maya asked.

Gus nodded and stopped a few yards away from a group of what looked like females if the pouches on their stomachs were anything to go by. 'I wouldn't go near a kangaroo that hasn't had human exposure. Too dangerous. Bucks, especially, can get violent, but females carrying a joey can lash out too,' he said, untying the knot in his calico bag. Some roo heads turned, large ears twitching. 'We raised a joey some time back. She comes to say hi a fair bit and others tag along.' Gus pulled out one of his grevillea plants. The sight of the bright red flower set a couple of the animals hopping in their direction.

Gus seemed relaxed enough, but Maya stepped in behind him. The kangaroos were used to seeing him out here in the paddocks. She, however, was a new entity and didn't want to take any chances in case they took a dislike to the colour of her T-shirt or the fact she smelled like a frog pond.

A smaller female came close enough to take a nibble on the flower and Maya peeked around Gus's shoulders. The next moment the roo reached for the whole branch, tugged it out of Gus's hand and proceeded to stuff its face with the flower head. Maya pushed her chin out to the side. Okay, so maybe he hadn't been lying about the kangaroos liking sea spray grevillea.

'Your turn.' Gus tipped his chin at the second roo hopping in their direction.

Maya blinked at his words and fished around in her calico bag. *Here goes nothing.* She stepped out from behind Gus and held out the plant. The roo didn't need to be asked twice to take a bite. Jaws working away, it didn't even break rhythm to come in for another serve.

Up this close, the animals really were impressive—their faces a little like a rabbit's but more serious, eyes darker, expressions fiercer. Even the females were muscle-wrapped and sinewy.

A third roo joined the two already chomping away at the grevillea. This time Maya didn't hesitate in offering it a feed. She was doing it! She was hand feeding a kangaroo! The corners of a smile dug deep into her cheeks. She turned to look at Gus and found him watching her, a smile of his own front and centre across his features.

'Thank you,' she whispered. In part, because she didn't want to startle the kangaroos, but also, because emotion suddenly closed up her throat and tugged her to the alley at the back of her father's garage …

'We should call the pound,' she'd told Michael as he crouched next to the dumpster. 'It could be dangerous.'

'Or it could just be lost and hungry.' Michael held out half of his pastrami cheese sandwich. The stray dog didn't have to be asked twice. It

devoured the bread in one desperate gulp, then dared to edge out a little from behind the dumpster, eyes big and brown and pleading.

Michael smiled at her and held out the other half of his sandwich. 'Your turn.'

'I'll admit, being here, like this, is kinda cool,' Gus said, pulling another grevillea head from his bag, 'but I still think you should swap some of your list items for ones a bit less ...' he gave her a sideways look from beneath raised eyebrows, '... cheesy.'

Maya rolled her eyes. 'Like what?'

Gus's face lit up like a rewired dashboard. 'Play some backyard cricket. Eat fresh mango till the juice drips down your chin. Jump off a rope swing into a waterhole.'

All those sounded worth checking out, but ... Nope. 'The list has to stay as is,' she said, a non-negotiable full stop at the end of her sentence.

Brow furrowed, Gus angled his head to look at her. 'I don't get it. Why is this so important to you?'

The sun was now high enough that its bottom brushed the horizon. Maya blinked into the glare, trying to find clarity amidst all her foggy emotion. Should she trust him? She was ninety-nine percent sure he'd planned for this morning to be a disaster, but now the sun seemed to burn away the shadows of what went before, and left Maya confused by the sincerity in Gus's eyes.

She filled her lungs with the sun-kissed air. 'The list is my brother's.'

Gus's brows pulled towards his nose. 'As in, it's something he wants you to do?'

Maya shook her head. 'It's something *he* always wanted to do.'

'So why isn't he the one standing here feeding kangaroos?'

'Because he's dead.'

Gus's face caved under the impact of the foot in his mouth. Maybe Maya could have delivered that titbit of information a little less brutally, but she'd been up since before the yawn of dawn and had an undignified dunking while everyone else was still cuddling their pillow. She really couldn't be arsed with subtlety at the moment. Also, there was satisfaction in seeing Gus scramble for an appropriate response.

'I'm sorry,' he eventually managed. So much for originality. 'I didn't know …' He looked into the calico bag, shook it like he was searching for something inside other than what was left of the flowers. 'How long ago?'

'A bit over a year.' The words still didn't come easy.

The roo closest to Gus started grabbing at his bag. Gus pulled another grevillea out and absentmindedly gave it to the animal. 'I'm sorry if I sounded … you know, flippant.'

Maya flicked him a tight smile. 'You didn't know.' Which was the way Maya had wanted it. It had been bad enough with everyone tiptoeing around her this past year at school.

Gus raked a hand through his hair, left it resting at the back of his neck as he glanced at Maya. He was wondering. Cancer? Car accident? Heart attack? He couldn't help it. Everyone who found out about Michael wondered. Maybe it was some weird evolutionary self-preservation thing, wanting to know how people died. Like it might help them avoid the same fate, or something.

Over the past twelve months Maya had learned to recognise the look of morbid curiosity on people's faces. The slightly pinched lips like they were working hard to keep the question from slipping out; the wide and startled but hungry-for-details eyes; the vague relief that they were the ones wondering instead of having to carry the crushing knowledge of how someone close to them had died. At the start, she'd hated that look. Now, it just made her tired.

Maya steeled herself. 'Bee sting. It was the first time and Michael went into anaphylactic shock. We didn't know he was allergic.' It'd been over a year now, but saying the words out loud still made her throat close over. She swallowed past the thickness.

'I was stressing out over a stupid history quiz I'd just done. It was

107

a Friday. Good day to take Big Bird out for a drive, Michael decided. To take my mind off school he'd said. So we took off on interstate 94, windows down, music up, me all bent out of shape about how school was stressing me out. And Michael ... he had a patient set of ears, and for someone who didn't say a lot, he always had the right words.' Maya brushed the leather cord on her wrist. 'We'd been driving for about an hour when the fan belt busted. Michael went to fix it and that's when the bee stung him.' Ten minutes later, he lay gasping for breath in her lap, hand clutching hers in a grip that was crushing— until it wasn't.

She rubbed the tips of her fingers on her palm trying to rid herself of the feeling. Maya sucked air into creaky lungs and pulled out another flower head. The two roos in front of her jostled for the feed.

She looked up, expecting pity in Gus's expression. What she saw was quiet understanding. *He gets it.* The day Patrick had come off his bike would have forced Gus through a similar maelstrom of emotions. Fear and disbelief and guilt. Such heavy guilt—because she couldn't follow Michael's simple instructions, couldn't do what he needed her to do.

Maya rubbed the knot dangling from her wrist. 'This was his.' She smiled down at the thin leather cord and nodded. 'It held together this battered old A5 notebook he used as a diary.' All his thoughts and fears and dreams bound tightly like a precious final gift. 'The list was on the first page.'

'It must have been hard to read it after ...' Gus trailed off but kept his eyes on her.

'I haven't read past the first few entries.'

Gus frowned. Her parents hadn't understood either. 'I read one entry a week. That way, I share in a day of his life a little bit at a time, stretching it out, making it last, discovering something new about him over time. If I read it all in one go, there'll be nothing left of him to discover.' This way he'd be with her for the next seven years at least. She gripped the leather wristband, pulled at it to make sure it was secure.

Slowly, Gus nodded like he understood. He fished another flower from his bag, fed it to the closest roo, then shoved the bag in his pocket. He held out his empty hands to the roos.

'I'm sorry. For badmouthing your brother's list and for being a right bastard since the day you arrived.' He turned to her, an apology in his eyes. 'From now on no more piss takes or talk of clichés, and I'll help you complete every item. I promise.'

'Even eat some Vegemite?'

Gus pretended to gag. 'I said I'd help *you* complete every item. I'm not going anywhere near that poison. Besides which, you've already ticked that off.'

Maya shook her head and grinned. Anyone would think she just asked him to spread engine oil on his toast. She felt around for another grevillea but came up empty.

'That's me done too.' She folded up the calico bag and popped it in her pocket, then held out her empty hands to the two roos in front of her like Gus had done.

'Better get going.' Gus motioned behind him to the house. 'Before these guys start ripping into our pockets for more food.'

They walked in silence, feet crunching through patches of dirt and grass, the sun now high enough to whip them with the day's first real sting. Maya caught sight of herself in the reflection of one of the homestead's windows. Mud streaked T-shirt, ratty ponytail that could have passed for one of the tufts of grass in the roo paddock, and … *What were those strings of black pearly things on— Eww! Gross!* Maya brushed the frog eggs off her shoulder. The slimy reminder of her dunking almost fouled her mood again. But no, she wouldn't allow herself to go there. Dip in the pond or not, she'd achieved what she'd wanted: ticking off another item on Michael's *List*. And strangely, now that she'd shared the reason behind the list with Gus, Maya didn't feel so alone in the venture anymore.

As they climbed the steps to the back door, she caught him looking at her. Something in his eyes had shifted, changed.

She looked away before the prickle of heat under her skin started Gus asking a whole set of other questions.

♡

The back door suddenly swung open and Jen's smiling face appeared. 'Where did the two of you get to so early?' Her eyes landed on Maya and widened.

'Gus took me to feed the kangaroos.' Maya tugged self-consciously on her T-shirt, which only drew more of Jen's attention to its wrecked state. Her mouth opened, probably to ask why Maya looked like she'd been dragged through a mud-filled watering trough, but she closed it again, and waved them both in. *Thank God.*

Wisely, Gus kept his mouth shut as he slunk into the kitchen behind her. He beelined for the fridge, but his mother stopped him with a hand on his elbow. 'Go see your father first. He wants to talk to you about some fencing that needs mending out in the top paddock. I'll get breakfast started.'

Shoulders sagging, he threw the fridge a longing look. 'I'll have some eggs if you're frying,' he said, turning for the hallway. 'And strong coffee.' His gaze found Maya's. 'I didn't get much sleep last night,' he added.

Suddenly, the scratches on the kitchen table had Maya's undivided attention. She really should apologise for the huntsman and accusing him of making the whole grevillea thing up to drag her out of bed so early.

The rising drone of the kettle boiling pulled Maya out of her thoughts and back into the kitchen. 'What can I do to help?'

Jen ran her gaze over Maya's ruined T-shirt. 'How about you go have a quick shower and then we'll talk about how you can help.'

Maya, too, glanced down at her semi-sodden self. 'Good idea.' She turned for the bathroom.

When she walked back into the kitchen a quarter of an hour later, Jen pointed to a wire basket on the sideboard full of eggs. 'Grab two of those for Gus and me and some for yourself,' she said, placing several mugs on the kitchen counter. 'Did you get many roos braving a hand feed this morning?'

'Three.' Maya carefully carried the eggs over to the stove top. 'All females. They liked the grevillea flowers Gus suggested we feed them.'

'Sea spray?'

Maya nodded.

'They do love the stuff. We practically raised an orphaned joey on the plant a while back.' Jen pulled a frying pan from the metal rack above them. 'Had it growing all through the back garden until the roos demolished the bushes to the point where there was hardly anything left.'

No wonder the Tinklers had theirs fenced off.

'I've now only got one bush left.'

Maya's head whipped in Jen's direction. 'You've got one left?'

'On the west side of the house where the dogs sleep.' Jen's brows pinched. 'Isn't that where you got the flowers?'

Maya froze. There'd been a bush here all along. With no fences to climb. No spindly shrubs to land in. No pond to fall into.

She forced herself to nod. 'Right, on the west side of the house.' She clenched her jaw. *Oh, he was good.*

But she was better.

Maya picked up an egg, cracked it against the side of the pan—hard. Egg white hissed and sizzled, taking shape alongside her revenge. 'You know, I think I'll have some more Vegemite toast instead of eggs, if that's okay. I might be developing a taste for it.'

Jen looked across at her, impressed. 'It's in the cupboard to your left.'

Maya spotted the large jar and smiled. Farmer Boy liked to play games, did he? Fine. Maya was about to play dirty.

Very, very dirty.

Chapter Twenty

Gus leaned on the fence post he'd just replaced and closed his eyes for a bit. The heat plus his lack of sleep made this fence repair more tedious than usual. Add Maya's revelation from earlier this morning and he was struggling to concentrate on the job.

Was she haunted by that afternoon? Did she relive it over and over, torturing herself with 'if onlys' that may have made all the difference—or may have made none? The weight of that Friday afternoon must be heavy. It would have crushed him well before now.

He wished Maya had explained the reason behind the list when she'd first arrived. He wouldn't have scoffed at her need to cuddle a koala if he'd known what motivated it. Would he still have gone ahead with his plan to run her off the farm? Probably not. Knowing and going ahead would have been a real shitty thing to do.

He thought of the Bluey in her bed, the rubber snake under the quad, and cringed. He couldn't undo what was already done, but he could make sure Maya ticked off the remaining items on that list. Strange, really, but somewhere between the lizard and the rubber snake, he'd started enjoying spending time with the girl from the Windy City. And if the huntsman was anything to go by, she was off plotting revenge after her morning dip in the fishpond instead of planning their Sydney trip with his mother. He should have insisted she came with them to mend the fence. God only knew what waited for him when he got back to the house.

He squinted into the sun, his growing grin only half catching him by surprise. Truth was, he was looking forward to seeing what she'd cooked up to get back at him.

'Gus!'

'Yeah!' Gus jerked in the direction of his father's voice.

His old man frowned at him. 'I said, hand me the wire strainers.'

Gus bent to pick up the tool—and to escape his father's annoyed glare. But the old man was justified. Slacking off on this job could result in nasty cuts thanks to snapped wires.

Like Gus needed any more reasons not to become a sheep farmer.

Gus watched his father clip the wire strainers onto the newly threaded fence. Practised precision. He made it look so easy. And maybe, for him, it was. For Gus, not so much.

'Not much sleep last night?' The old man didn't look up from his work, but his eyebrows pushed down towards his nose in concern.

Gus yawned on cue.

His father grunted. 'Never liked huntsmen.'

Really? According to all the lectures Gus'd heard over the years, spiders were a godsend cause they kept the mosquitos down.

'Don't mind the smaller ones, even the funnel webs.' His father twisted the fence wire round and round itself, snipped the end with some pliers. 'But the big ones creep me out. Don't blame you for not wanting to sleep in your room.'

About to pull the wire strainer off the fence, Gus paused and looked at his father's stern profile. It wasn't like the old man to admit to a fear. A reminder that even his tough-as-an-old-drizabone dad had weaknesses if you looked hard enough.

Gus whacked the wire strainer from the fence and clipped it on the next bit of slack wire that needed replacing. 'Did you know Maya's brother died a year ago?'

A frown, then a grunt. Gus took that as a no. 'Bee sting allergy,' he continued. 'Maya was with him when it happened.'

This time his father looked up and Gus swore he saw the memory of a quad bike flipping flash across his father's features. For a beat, the man's face crumpled like tissue paper, then his gaze quickly returned to the wire fence—to safe territory.

Fear wasn't the only emotion Gus's father didn't like showing. He was Switzerland when it came to emotions. Publicly neutral. Anything that might expose a softer side was kept well under wraps. There was a farm to run.

But sometimes Gus wondered ... 'You ever want to be something other than a farmer, Dad?'

His old man's hand stuttered in its round and round wire coiling rhythm—but only briefly. Gus waited for the look, the one that said *are-you-out-of-your-sheep-farming-mind*? Instead, his dad gazed up over the water-starved land, eyes brushing the groups of faraway grey-white specks moving about in the paddocks. 'Why would I, when farming gives me all this?' He turned to Gus and smiled for the first time that day.

Gus's shoulders sagged. *That about seals it.* His father simply couldn't comprehend a life without the land. He honestly thought he was doing the best thing he could for his son by having him follow in his footsteps. Just like his father had before him, and his father's father before that.

For Richard Robertson, there was no nobler life than that of a sheep farmer, and as much as Gus resented his father for forcing him down the same path, in a warped way he also loved the man for wanting to pass on his passion. Even if Gus would never appreciate it the way he did.

The snap of the wire strainers coming off the fence pulled Gus out of his thoughts and back to the job that needed doing. Back to the sheep-filled life that caged his future like the fencing that contained everything his father loved.

He picked up the ream of coil and followed his father to the next stretch of fencing in need of re-wiring. Seemed he was destined to follow in the old man's footsteps in every way.

Chapter Twenty-One

'Before I book this bridge climb, how are you with heights?' Jen looked across the kitchen table at Maya, fingers pausing over her laptop keyboard.

'I'm good with heights.' She'd been to the top of Wills Tower like everyone else in Chicago.

Jen beamed at her. A couple of keyboard taps later, she turned the laptop on the kitchen table so Maya could see the screen better. 'It's really spectacular. Richard bought me a Sydney Harbour Bridge climb for our last anniversary.' She pointed at the screen and all of the different climbing options. 'We'll have to see how it fits in with the Opera House show, but if we can manage it, I think you should do the twilight climb. That's the one we did.' Jen's eyes crinkled with a smile. 'It really was magical.'

Maya poured over the pictures on the laptop. People in dorky grey-blue jumpsuits, massive grins on their faces, the Sydney skyline lit up behind them.

Just the kind of thing Michael would have loved doing. 'If you don't mind doing it again, I'd really like to do the twilight climb.'

Jen pulled the laptop back her way and clicked on the booking tab. 'I certainly wouldn't mind doing it again, but I was hoping to catch up with some old friends on Saturday night. I don't get to

Sydney that often, so it'll only be you and Gus climbing the bridge. If you don't mind?' She raised hopeful brows at Maya.

'No, no. Of course I don't mind.' But Maya squirmed on her seat. There was the very real danger she'd push Gus off the bridge. Only fair after what he did this morning. Or maybe not so much, once he found the little surprise waiting in his room. Maya bit her lip to keep from grinning too widely.

'Now, the Opera House. What kind of show would you like to see?' Jen turned the laptop Maya's way again and raised her brows expectantly.

Turns out there was more to see at the Opera House than just opera. Drama, jazz, ballet, musical theatre, comedy, some kids' play based on a book she'd never heard of, even a lecture on the wonders of jellyfish. They'd looked at the entire Opera House program this morning, but Maya was still overwhelmed. She tugged on a wannabe curl before sliding it behind her ear. What would Michael have chosen to see?

The obvious choice was comedy, but would he have chosen something else, something totally unexpected?

She scrolled through the program one more time. 'Let's do the Graeme Murphy one.' Maya pointed at the tutu-and-leotard-clad dancers contorted into pretzel-like positions. A ballet. She and Michael had only ever been to one. Maybe this time she'd manage to sit still instead of fidgeting throughout the entire performance.

Jen broke out in a huge smile. 'I'm so glad you said that. I've always wanted to see a Graeme Murphy production, and this version of *The Nutcracker* is meant to be very good. And it's not something Richard would sit through.' She pulled up the booking page and started looking for tickets.

Maya put a hand on Jen's to stop her. 'Wait, is ballet something Gus would want to sit through?' Ballet wasn't for everyone.

'Why don't we ask him,' Jen said, swivelling to face the hallway where boots clomped down the hardwood floors.

Gus's father was the first to come into the kitchen. He pulled his hat off and ran a leathery hand through dusty hair. 'That's the top paddock fence fixed.' He filled a glass with water and downed it in four greedy gulps. 'There's another stretch in the adjoining lot that looks like it'll need some work, but it can wait for a few weeks.' He tipped his hat at the laptop screen in front of Jen. 'How's the Sydney planning going?'

Jen smiled at her husband. 'Almost organised. We only need Gus to tell us if he'll come and see Graeme Murphy's ballet with us.' She looked at Gus as he walked into the kitchen behind his father.

'Graeme Murphy?' Gus, too, removed his hat and beelined for the sink and some water. 'Isn't he that footballer who posted a YouTube video of his drunk dog?'

Maya snorted but kept quiet.

Jen shook her head and sighed. 'The Graeme Murphy we're seeing is a well-known choreographer,' she said. 'And I very much doubt he'd be putting videos of his dog, drunk or otherwise, on YouTube.'

'Shame.'

Maya bit her lip at the disappointment in Gus's voice. 'Does that mean you won't be seeing *The Nutcracker* with us?'

Throat working as he swallowed, Gus peered at her over the top of his water glass. She could almost see the cogs and wheels turning in his head as he tried to come up with a valid reason not to go with them.

'Can't imagine Gus'll want to see a ballet,' Mr Robertson said, opening the fridge. 'Maybe he can catch up with the boys for a surf. Make up for missing the trip.'

Head stuck in the fridge and back to everyone, the man couldn't see Gus narrowing his eyes on a spot somewhere between his father's shoulders. Maya totally understood Gus's annoyance. A day surfing would never make up for missing a whole six weeks of—she straightened in her chair. If Pat didn't know then ... the Robertsons also had no idea where Gus had really planned to spend the summer.

She snagged Gus's gaze. Eyes wide and a little frantic, he gave a tiny shake of his head—a silent plea to keep quiet.

'It'd be a hassle to take the surfboard up for one day,' Gus said, putting his glass on the kitchen sink. 'I'll come see the ballet.'

Maya kept staring Gus's way, questions burning the whites of her eyes.

'I'm gonna grab a shower,' he said. As he passed, he looked up, mouthed the word 'later' to Maya, then disappeared down the hallway with long, hurried strides.

Chapter Twenty-Two

The minute he stepped out of the shower, Gus knew he needed to come completely clean. With Maya, that was. Yes, he'd apologised for scoffing at her list and for treating her badly, but she deserved more—a gesture or truce of some sort. He was surprised she hadn't ratted him out just now in the kitchen. Instead, she'd kept his secret.

He wiped the condensation from the mirror. Like his water-smudged reflection, things had come into focus. Maya deserved an answer to all those question marks that'd popped up all over her face at the mention of the surfing trip. Today. He'd explain everything today. That, and apologise for *all* his antics over the past few days. Now that he knew the reason behind Maya's list, there was no way he could keep trying to run her off the farm. He kinda enjoyed having her around anyway.

Gus quit rubbing the towel over his hair and found his frowning face in the mirror. When exactly did he go from wanting her gone to *kinda enjoying* having her around? He pulled a face at his reflection. What did it matter? Simple truth was, he didn't mind the idea of spending the rest of the summer helping her complete her brother's list. Not like he'd be able to use whatever he'd have learned at the CGI summer school anyway.

As soon as he entered his room, Gus scanned the walls and

ceiling for an eight-legged trespasser. He hadn't seen the huntsman since last night, so the critter had likely scurried outside in search of his next insect meal. But there was also the chance the crafty not-so-little bugger was lurking in a shadowy crevice somewhere, ready to scare the sunburn off his skin. Man, he hated spiders. Hated them. It made him appreciate Maya's quiet genius in hiding one in his underwear drawer all the more.

Pulling clean clothes out of his cupboard, he shook his head, a smile snaking its way across his face. Their unspoken back-and-forth revenge pranks would now come to an end. Pity. He'd have liked to have seen her next move.

Once dressed, Gus sat on his bed to pull on his boots. Unfortunately, his work day wasn't over yet. His father was interviewing for a couple of new farm hands and he wanted Gus to sit in, since he'd be the one doing the hiring in the future.

Gus sighed and reached down to grab his Blundstones when he whiffed something. Bit like … off mushrooms? Fungus-y. Yeasty.

Nasty.

He checked the bottom of the shoes. Nothing. Sniffed his T-shirt. Nah, that wasn't it either. Maybe he should have taken a bit longer in the shower? But a quick whiff under his armpits confirmed he'd scrubbed everything well enough.

So what on earth was it?

His eyes widened. Ralph! The last time the dopey dog had killed something and dragged it in here to hide, it'd taken Gus weeks to get rid of the putrid dead possum smell. Dropping to his knees, Gus squinted into the dusty shadows under his bed, fully prepared to find the rotting carcass of some poor furry animal festering on a pile of dust bunnies.

But again … nothing. Except the smell was definitely coming from down here.

'Huh.' He pushed up off the floor and grabbed his boots, ready to tug them on again, when something red caught his eye on his bed.

Make that under his bedspread, sticking out just near his pillow.

A grevillea.

A sea spray grevillea to be exact.

Gus's brows drew together as he pulled the limp red flower from under his bedspread. He'd fed all of his flowers to the roos, so had Maya …

His head snapped up, eyes finding his bedroom window—and the dog shed behind which Mum's grevillea was blooming nicely for this time of year.

Maya. She must have found the sea spray bush, realised there'd been no need for the trip to the neighbouring farm, and planted this little flower as a warning.

Lips twitching, Gus brushed the red bristles with his thumb. He couldn't wait to see what she'd cook up to get back at him. First, though, he had to get going and meet his father.

A couple of sharp tugs and his boots were on. Up off the bed, Gus beelined for the door but something felt … off. His feet felt … weird, like he had mud between his toes.

He grabbed hold of the bedframe, pulled off one boot and his mouth fell open. His foot was black, like he'd stepped into a bucket of engine grease or tar or …

Vegemite.

Gus closed his mouth to calm his gagging reflex. He wriggled the toes of his other foot and … yeah, both boots. Probably a whole jar's worth of the black poison. He shuddered, gagged again.

Then grinned.

Bloody brilliant.

He'd underestimated Maya. She was way craftier at this revenge prank thing than he'd thought.

Gus tucked his chin into his chest and held his breath as he pulled the boot back on. He'd squelch his way to the bathroom to clean this disaster up, do the interviews with his father, then find Maya and wave a white flag in surrender.

'You got a minute?'

Maya looked up from Emmy's latest baking video on her laptop to find Gus leaning against her doorway, all Friday afternoon casual in a pair of laze-about drawstring shorts and a well-loved grey cotton tee. She blinked. This Gus was so unlike the uptight outback cowboy she'd met her first day here. The clothes weren't the only point of difference. There was something else about him standing there all cleaned-up and relaxed. Maybe it was his hair, a couple of locks at the front defying his recent attempt to comb it off his face, or the promise of a smile playing at the corners of his lips, or the way he angled his head a little, somehow softening his already softly spoken question. Whatever it was, Maya no longer felt a need to be wary around Gus Robertson. She no longer felt … unwelcome. Which unsettled and confused her to no end.

She offered him a cautious smile. 'What's up?'

'I was wondering, do you want to watch a movie?'

A movie? With her? He obviously hadn't found her Vegemite surprise yet. Wait, maybe he had and this was all part of his retaliation plan. Lure her into a false sense of security watching a movie, then *bam!* She's eating deep-fried cockroaches instead of popcorn.

She narrowed her eyes at him. 'You want to watch a movie? With me?'

A nod. 'I thought we could, you know—' he waved a hand back and forth between them, '—hang out.'

Hang out? He wants to hang out? Like he hadn't spent all his energy trying to get rid of her since she'd first arrived? Maya looked him up and down for an ulterior motive, but if he had one, it was hard to see behind the openly hopeful expression on his face.

Damn. There was a sucker born every minute and clearly her minute had just clocked over.

She wriggled to sit higher on her bed. 'Do I get to pick the movie?'

Gus's shoulders visibly relaxed. He scratched his chin. 'As long as it's not some Disney princess sop fest, sure.'

Maya snorted. 'I spent the day elbow deep in quad bike parts. Do you really think I'd pick a Disney sop fest?'

Gus peered at her, lips puckering like he was weighing up her argument. 'Sure, but I get to pick the snacks.'

'Deal.' Maya closed her laptop and slid off her bed. Since he was the one more likely to know where snacks were kept in this house, she had no problem with the arrangement. And she knew exactly which movie she was going to pick.

They detoured via the kitchen where Maya nodded in silent approval as Gus grabbed a packet of salted caramel popcorn and a block of chocolate from the pantry (unopened—she checked). By the time they arrived in the living room, she was actually looking forward to the evening. If this was all part of an elaborate retaliation plan, she'd really be miffed.

Gus held the remote out to her. She went to take it, but he held on. 'No soppy romcoms either or I'm not sharing the popcorn,' he warned before letting go.

Maya shook her head. 'Trust me, you're in no danger of a soppy anything tonight.' Or any night, really. She had nothing against a bit of romance in her entertainment, but she'd never been a Disney kind of girl. Unless it involved talking robots or cars.

'You sure your mum won't mind us taking over the TV?' In the few days she'd been on the farm, Maya had quickly learned that Jen liked to kick back in front of the television at the end of a long day.

'Don't worry. *The Farmer Wants a Wife* isn't on tonight.' She thought she heard him mutter 'Thank God' under his breath but couldn't be sure; Gus had turned away to grab one of the cushions at the far end of the couch.

'Besides,' he said, wedging the cushion behind his back and popping his feet on the coffee table, 'Mum and Dad are out tonight. Country Women's Association fundraiser.'

'And Patrick?' She'd heard him pottering about in his room earlier. 'We should ask him if he wants to watch this with us.'

'I already did. He's busy with something else, apparently.' Gus snatched up the popcorn packet he'd dumped on the coffee table. 'So you going to pick a movie or what?'

Maya harrumphed and clicked through the menu on the screen until she came to the action adventure section. 'I've just spent half an hour trying to watch a ten minute YouTube video thanks to your last century wi-fi. You sure this is going to work?'

'Why do you think this is jumbo size?' Gus held up the popcorn packet. 'We'll get through at least a third of it while the movie downloads. Oh, and don't expect high definition. Choose your movie already.'

Maya shrugged. A quick scan down the menu and she found what she was looking for. 'How about this?'

'*Ready Player One?*' Gus quirked a surprised brow at her. 'Don't tell me you're one of those "bring back the eighties" tragics. I get enough of that from my parents.'

Maya sighed, all very dramatic and exaggerated. 'And here I thought you were starting to know me.' She pointed the remote control at the screen and selected the movie. 'It's all about the cars and race scenes for me, cowboy.'

Gus shook his head but grinned as he tore open the popcorn and tipped his chin at the TV for her to start the movie.

'And the CGI is out of this world,' she added, slowly angling up a brow at him.

He froze, eyes finding hers then quickly sliding away. 'Yeah, about that. Thanks for not saying anything in front of my parents.'

Maya lowered the remote into her lap. 'Why haven't you told them about the summer school?'

'It's com—'

'—and don't say it's complicated.'

Gus blew out a breath, drew his feet back onto the floor and peered across at Maya. 'Look, Mum and Dad don't know about the summer school because I don't want them thinking it's something I want to pursue.'

'Wait, I'm confused. I thought this was something you loved.'

'It is.'

'So why not tell them?'

Pain slashed across his face. 'Because it's not something my father approves of.'

Maya paused at that. 'Have you actually spoken to him about it?'

Gus snorted. 'He thinks anything to do with computer animation is just a bunch of people playing games, not a real job—a complete waste of time.'

He wasn't answering the question. 'But does he know how good you are at it? That you could make a living doing this, doing a job you love?'

Gus's lips flattened into a resigned line. 'It's already been decided how I'll be making my living. Whether I love it or not is beside the point. My family needs me on the farm.'

His future had already been decided? *My family needs me …*

Patrick.

The accident.

'You're going to take over the farm for Patrick.'

Gus nodded. A simple dip of the head, but it looked like one of the most painful things he'd ever done.

Maya's instinct urged her to reach out to him; to offer him something in the way of comfort. Instead, she drew back further into her corner of the couch. Right now, Gus reminded her of a cornered animal, trapped and frustrated by his circumstances. Her touch, even a sudden movement, might send him retreating back into himself. She didn't want that. What she wanted was for him to keep talking, to continue giving her a glimpse into the real Gus, the one who felt the need to hide such a pivotal part of himself from the people who loved him most.

'Is this what Patrick wants?' she prodded gently. 'Because only yesterday Patrick told me he wanted to be more involved with the running of the farm. Maybe he could—'

'How?' Gus threw up his hands, almost knocking over the packet of popcorn. 'To run a farm this size you need to be mobile, Maya, and no matter how much Pat wants to help, at the end of the day, there's only so much he can do trapped in a damn wheelchair.'

The outburst had Maya freezing. Gus immediately whipped his head around to the door, eyes wide and fearful that his brother might have heard the harsh words.

Maya leaned forward, caught Gus's gaze with hers when he turned back her way. 'There are ways he could be more mobile. A few alterations to the quad bike and a hoist to help him get into it would—'

'No.' The word was filled with horror and Gus's face paled much like it had yesterday in the machinery shed. 'There's no way Pat's ever getting back on a quad bike. It's hard enough controlling one of those things when you've got use of all your limbs let alone when …' He heaved a sigh. 'No. There's just no way. Not when I can do what needs to be done around here.' He grabbed the remote from Maya's lap and stabbed it at the TV to start the movie. Conversation over.

Maya wouldn't let herself be shut down so easily. 'Have you ever asked Patrick if he wants you to step in for him?'

'What he wants doesn't matter. We're both trapped thanks to that wheelchair of his,' Gus snapped. Maya flinched.

'I'm sorry.' Expression crumbling, he reached out a hand as though to touch her, but stopped, and handed her the remote instead. 'Can we please just watch the movie and not talk about this?' His eyes pleaded with her to let it go.

Maya exhaled a shaky breath. She'd opened a sticky can of worms. One that had her thinking maybe she should keep nice and quiet about her promise to help Patrick modify his quad bike. From the locked line of Gus's jaw, Maya suspected he wouldn't be too receptive to Patrick's side of the argument right at this moment.

So she clicked *play*. The wi-fi was in a good mood and they watched the opening credits in awkward silence.

Until Gus suddenly grabbed the remote from her and hit *pause*.

'Maya, I'm sorry,' he said, turning to face her.

She frowned. 'You've already said that.'

'I know, and I am sorry for losing my shit just now. But all this ...' he waved a hand over the popcorn, the couch, the TV, '... this was meant to be an apology for the last few days, and here I've gone and stuffed it up before the movie's even started.' He speared both hands through his hair, frustration creasing his brow as he looked across at her.

Maya leaned forward in her seat. 'Apology for the last few days?' Was he going to admit to trying to run her off the farm?

He rubbed the back of his neck. 'The Blue Tongue, the rubber snake ...'

Maya's eyes widened. He was owning up to it all. 'And the 4 am grevillea trip?'

Gus winced. 'Yeah, and the 4 am grevillea trip.'

Maya crossed her arms. 'The Blue Tongue was evil.'

'Not as evil as the huntsman.' Gus gave her a death stare.

'I can't take all the credit for the huntsman.' Maya reached for the open packet of popcorn Gus had abandoned. 'Your brother was the mastermind there.'

Gus sighed and nodded in silent acknowledgement, maybe even a little respect. 'Figured as much. But I bet the underwear drawer was your idea.'

'Guilty as charged.'

Gus shook his head at Maya's triumphant grin. 'You jump the moment a sheep brushes against you. How are you not scared of spiders?'

She shrugged. 'Dad's workshop was always full of crawling critters. I wouldn't go getting a spider as a pet, but they don't freak me out like they do most people. Snakes, on the other hand …' She shuddered and popped some corn into her mouth, glaring at Gus. 'It almost sent me packing, which is exactly what you wanted, right?' She cocked a brow in challenge.

Lips clamped tightly together, Gus nodded.

Something in Maya deflated. Stupid, really. She'd had all the evidence, and now that she knew the significance of the Sydney summer school, in a weird way she understood why Gus wanted her gone. Still, a small part of her had been hoping he'd tell her she had it all wrong.

'I'm not proud of myself,' Gus said, looking suitably apologetic. 'It's just, when I overheard your phone call to your friend, I figured you'd be more than happy to have a reason for leaving this Hicksville backwater.'

Maya bit her lip. 'That's right, you heard that.'

Gus pulled back to peer at her from underneath scrunched brows. 'How do you know I heard that?'

'I went looking for you after the rubber snake episode,' Maya said. 'Your whole snake-falling-from-the-rafters story was off. I was going to confront you, get you to admit you were responsible for all the strange animal encounters. That's when I found the cage in your room … and overheard you telling Patrick you'd heard me call Barrangaroo Creek a Hicksville backwater.'

'Which is when you decided to go hunting for spiders.' Gus shook his head, a faint line of a smile ghosting over his face. 'For what it's worth, I felt like crap after the snake. I was planning on coming clean and apologising the next day, but then you planted the huntsman—'

'—After which you plotted the disastrous and totally unnecessary grevillea trip.' Maya crossed her arms.

'Minus the dog. I swear I didn't know about the dog. And the pond was a bonu—'

Maya's glare cut him off.

'—accident! The pond was an accident.' Gus had the decency to look sorry—for about a second. 'But yeah, the 4am trip was unnecessary. Which is why you decided the inside of my boots needed to be decorated with Vegemite.'

Maya fought to contain her grin. She lost. 'I don't understand why you turn your nose up at the stuff. It's delicious. I felt you just needed an opportunity to …' she circled a hand in front of Gus's face in an encouraging gesture, ' …really immerse yourself in the essence of it.'

'I bet you did.' Gus lost his own battle keeping a straight face. Then it suddenly turned serious and he looked down at his hands in his lap. 'All jokes aside, I'm done trying to scare you off the farm. It was a stupid and selfish thing to do, and I'm not proud of it.' He shifted on the couch, found her eyes with his. 'We're heading off to Sydney tomorrow and I want us to start again, as friends, because I meant what I said this morning, I want to help you finish your list. No more stunts, Maya, I promise.' Gaze locked on hers, he held out his hand. 'Truce?'

Maya looked at Gus's outstretched fingers, at the offer of friendship they held, and sat up straighter. As entertaining as her revenge pranks on him had been, she really could use a friend to help her finish Michael's list.

'Truce,' she said, sliding her hand into his. They shook, gazes locked for a fraction longer than was necessary. Maya broke eye contact first.

Gus cleared his throat. 'So you've cuddled a koala, fed a kangaroo and eaten some Vegemite toast. We're climbing the Harbour Bridge and seeing a show at the Opera House this weekend. What else was on that list?'

'The didgeridoo. Your dad said we might be able to do that in Sydney as well?'

'We might,' Gus said.

'And sleep out under the Southern Cross.'

Gus scratched his chin. 'I have an idea for that one when we get back.'

Maya smiled and hugged the pillow in her lap. She was liking this new, amicable version of Gus.

The next two hours passed in a blur of salted caramel popcorn, the odd debate over eighties trivia and a few explanations of computer-generated animation that went right over Maya's head. When he wasn't surly or trying to land her in a frog-egg infested pond, Gus was actually okay to hang out with. He didn't hog the couch, made sure to ask if she wanted the last piece of chocolate, and didn't laugh when she sang along to the thirty-year-old soundtrack.

By the end of the night, Maya was looking forward to the Sydney trip, safe in Gus's promise not to run her off the farm.

Here was hoping he wasn't one to go back on his promises.

Chapter Twenty-Three

'Did you just say you love *MacGyver*?'

Maya cut Gus a narrow-eyed look in the rearview mirror. 'According to my brother, *MacGyver* is essential life skill viewing.' Her voice dared him to argue. She thought she heard a scoff from the back seat, but it was hard to tell over the creaks and groans of the old station wagon as Jen sped down the highway.

According to the little dot on Maya's GPS, they were an hour or so away from Sydney. Jen had kicked off the Q-and-A about Maya's life back in Chicago shortly after leaving Barangaroo Creek, but not long after they'd hit the highway, Gus was the one peppering Maya with get-to-know-you questions.

'Ah, I get it. It's one of those family bonding experiences. Bit like *The Farmer Wants a Wife* is for Mum, Ruth and Pat.'

This time it was Jen who cut Gus the narrow-eyed look.

But he wasn't far off. Watching *MacGyver* had very much been Maya's time with Michael.

'Are we talking the remake or the original?'

Maya snorted. 'The original. Michael watched one episode of the remake and declared it dead on arrival. For him, there is only one Angus MacGyver.' She swivelled in her seat and grinned at the Angus sitting behind her. 'You should give the show a try since the main character is your namesake.'

'Pass.' Gus offered a humourless smile. 'There's only so many times I'm willing to watch someone defuse a bomb with a paperclip before it gets boring.'

'Shows how much you know.' She turned back to face the front. 'The paperclip is only one tool in MacGyver's vast arsenal. He's a master at using what's at hand. In one episode he plugs a sulphuric acid leak with chocolate.'

This time there was no mistaking Gus's scoff. 'Yeah, cause that's believable.'

'Actually, it is.' Maya threw a look over her shoulder.

'Really?' Jen asked.

'Yes, the acid reacts with the sugars and forms this thick gunky residue that blocks the leak. *Mythbusters* proved it.'

Jen nodded, clearly impressed.

A surprised *huh* came from the back seat. One point to Maya. Not that she was keeping track or anything, but she was enjoying this amicable sparring that underpinned her and Gus's banter.

She was also enjoying the trip down memory lane all the talk of *MacGyver* took her on. 'Michael was a real gadget and hack nut, his brain always whirring and solving problems. We watched the reruns on DVD Saturday nights whenever he wasn't out with his friends and I didn't have schoolwork to finish. It was our thing.' Curled up on the couch, sharing a tub of peanut butter crunch ice cream, trying to predict how MacGyver would make it out of his latest jam. Warmth spread through Maya's chest at the memory, followed by an ice-pick stab of grief.

Gus's tap on her shoulder tugged her off memory lane and back into the car. 'Confess, you ever give any of the tricks a go?'

'Once.' Maya bit her lip. 'It didn't end well.'

Gus stuck his head between the front seats, face turned towards her all animated with glee. 'This I gotta hear.'

The episode responsible for Maya's own MacGyvering flashed

before her mind and she squeezed her eyes shut. *The Thief of Budapest*. 'Let's just say my recipe of salt, sugar, chemically enhanced weed killer plus a few drops of battery acid blew a massive hole into half the kitchen cupboards.'

'For real?' Gus sounded suitably impressed.

'Mum was horrified I'd almost burned down the kitchen and I wasn't allowed near anything flammable for the next six months. Michael, of course, took me off to the workshop the moment my parents weren't looking and made me walk through the recipe again so I could figure out where I went wrong.'

'You and Michael must have been close.' Jen's voice was full of warmth and none of the pity she usually heard from people when they realised her brother was dead. But her comment was past tense, so she knew. Gus must have told her.

Maya nodded, her fingers reaching for the coolness of her leather band. 'Michael was four years old when Mum and Dad brought me home from hospital. Apparently, he took one frown-filled look at me, nodded in a much-too-serious way for a four-year-old, and said, "I'll look after her". That's exactly what he did from then on.'

And the one time I should have looked after him, I let him down.

Maya tugged on her seatbelt, lifting it from her suddenly too-tight chest. The sudden silence in the car amplified all the creaks and groans of the station wagon.

Gus's hand found her shoulder a second time. 'For what it's worth, I'm with Michael—give me a recipe with a bit of zing any day. Nothing worse than something bland coming out of the kitchen, don't you think, Mum?'

Maya caught Gus's wink in the rearview mirror as he sat back in his seat.

'Definitely,' Jen said, offering Maya another warm smile.

Maya relaxed into her seat. The turnoff to Sydney loomed up ahead. She smiled to herself—just enough time to teach Gus the *MacGyver* theme song.

Most people would shudder at the thought of putting on an ugly, full-body jumpsuit, matching cap included. Maya, however, couldn't wait. Wearing it meant she was one step closer to ticking off another item on Michael's list. And the fashion reject of a jumpsuit reminded her a little of the scrubby overalls Michael and her dad wore in the workshop. In a strange kind of way, she felt like she was taking a piece of her brother with her on this high-altitude adventure.

Their climb leader, Phil, waved to get their attention. 'Just a final reminder,' his tone as serious as his smile was wide, 'you can't carry anything on the climb with you. Even a small coin can become a big problem when dropped from the top of the bridge.' Then he reassured them that if his oldest climber—an arthritic ninety-three-year-old grandmother of twelve from Dunedoo called Beryl—could manage the climb, then their troupe would do just fine.

Maya's feet had a bad case of excited-foot-to-foot-shifting while Phil finished his safety spiel. She just wanted to get going already!

Finally, they connected their harnesses to a safety line along the rail and Phil led them single file along a metal walkway though a concrete tunnel.

'Have you climbed the Bridge before?' she asked Gus over her shoulder.

'No. This is my first time.'

An unexpected tension in Gus's voice had Maya frowning back at him. 'You're not scared of heights, are you?' They'd moved through the tunnel and now the metal walkway spat them out the side of one of the support pylons. The steel arches of the bridge loomed imposing and high in front of them.

'I'm good with heights.' He smiled at her when she glanced back at him again, but it was tight and somehow wrong. She didn't get a chance to ask him what the matter was, because he waved her forward across the next metal walkway, several yards above the growing Saturday evening traffic.

Massive girders suddenly snagged Maya's attention. They stretched hard and grey above them in all directions. All that steel. So many rivets—six million according to Phil's voice coming through her headset, some the size of her fist, some as big as her arm. She would have stopped to gape if she didn't have other climbers on her heels. They hadn't even started the climb and Maya was already geeking out on the construction. *Michael would have loved this!*

The blue-green water of the harbour stretched beneath them under the metal mesh of the horizontal walkway, until they reached a ladder at the foot of what she guessed to be the bridge's arch. Halfway up the ladder, a gust of wind threatened to blow off her regulation cap.

She glanced down at Gus behind her. He was paying close attention to where he was putting his feet, but wasn't showing any signs of clamming up or freaking out. In fact, when he looked up and caught her eye, he winked. *Huh.* Maybe she'd imagined the tension in his voice earlier.

Nothing prepared Maya for the summit of the Bridge.

With the sun minutes from dipping its toes into the horizon, the city lay bathed in twilight gold dust. Ferries cut ripples along the glass surface of the harbour and the Opera House sails flamed red in the dimming light. The whole 360-degree view was just—

'Spec-bloody-tacular.' Gus echoed her thoughts. He grinned at her. 'Dare you to do a Leonardo DiCaprio,' he said and wriggled his eyebrows.

'Don't tempt me.' She just might. There was something about being up this high that made you want to throw your hands in the air and scream 'I'm the king of the world' into the wind. But Maya was too awestruck, so they admired the view in silence for a little while.

'See over there?' Gus pointed behind them to their right. 'If you squint, you can just spot Bondi Beach.'

Maya followed his instructions but couldn't make out the beach they'd visited that morning.

'And there—' Gus pointed behind them to the left, '—past the wharves. Know what that is?'

Maya looked at the stretch of green he indicated. She shook her head. 'No idea.' What did she know about parklands in inner Sydney?

'That's Barangaroo reserve, part of the suburb of Barangaroo,' Gus said, turning to look with her.

Lush parklands and modern high-rises overlooked one of the world's most beautiful harbours. That's where she thought she'd spend her time in Sydney. On this amazing harbour, with this beautiful view spread out before her every day for six whole weeks.

'I get why you'd want to stay here instead of on a dusty old sheep farm.' A crooked smile pulled Gus's expression into something that resembled an apology.

'Photo time!' Phil's voice boomed through the headset. 'This here's the highest point of the Sydney Harbour Bridge, so show us your pearly whites for a happy snappy before the sun sets.'

Afterwards, Maya soaked up the city as they made their way back down the arch on the west side. The sun disappeared and the lights below flickered, rushing and converging as the city woke and stretched, ready to take on a Saturday night.

Did she still wish she could have spent her time here instead of on a dusty old farm like Barangaroo Creek? She cut Gus a quick glance—she wasn't sure anymore what she wanted.

It was close to eleven by the time Maya and Gus reached their hotel rooms and said their goodnights. Jen was fast asleep on her side of their shared room. Maya, however, was wide awake with post-climb adrenalin and snuck out on the balcony instead of climbing into her bed.

Below her, Circular Quay hummed with night life under the arch of the Harbour Bridge. She snapped a quick photo of the iconic view and uploaded it along with the one taken of the bridge summit to her feed. They loaded instantly. *Ah, the bliss of good internet reception.* She sent both pics to her parents. It was morning back home so a good chance someone was around to reply.

Her mother messaged back straight away, glad Maya was having a good time and reminding her to send photos of tomorrow's Opera House visit.

Emmy's comment on her post came not long after.

Wow! Talk about a stunning view!

Maya smiled. Emmy wouldn't climb a tree let alone the Sydney Harbour Bridge thanks to her dislike of heights.

She 'liked' the comment and replied with *AMAZING!*

Emmy's next comment came via private message.

Even though it means spending a weekend with Farmer Boy?

Maya grinned at her friend's question. She'd filled Emmy in on her huntsman and Vegemite revenge before the movie last night.

We've now called a truce. He's actually kind of okay to hang out with when he's not being a snake-planting jerk.

Maya's face warmed at those last words. Thankfully Em was not there to see it.

It took a while for Em's next message to appear. When it did, all she sent her way was a winking emoji.

Maya replied with an eye roll GIF—and a literal one.

Tomorrow was another day with another list item to tick.

Chapter Twenty-Four

Gus followed his mother and Maya out of the Opera House and let out a massive breath. 'And here I thought listening to you humming the *MacGyver* theme song in the car was bad.' Classical music for three hours was *much* worse.

'Oh, come on.' Maya's expression scrunched in exasperation. 'It wasn't that bad. There must've been something you enjoyed about the ballet?'

Something he enjoyed about the ballet … 'Hmm, let me think … the interval?'

His answer earned him a shove.

'You chose to come, remember?' his mother said.

Yeah, he did. And if he was honest, he was glad he came. The weekend so far had been way more enjoyable than he'd imagined.

He couldn't remember the last time he'd spent time away from the farm with Mum.

And then there was Maya, a bubble of excitement from the moment they checked into the hotel. Seeing Sydney through her eyes put a fresh spin on the city experience. Even the ballet. By the end of the first half, he'd been sucked into the Australian take on the Nutcracker story. His moaning and groaning was nothing but bait, really. For Maya. All those pranks he'd subjected her to had given him a taste for Maya with her hackles up.

'I chose to come, yes.' He sighed, hamming it up a bit more. 'But now I want to go and get something to eat. All that dancing makes a guy hungry.'

He was expecting another eye roll from Maya. Instead, he got two raised brows of interest.

'I could eat,' she said. 'Especially if there's something sweet involved.'

'Great.' Gus rubbed his hands together and upped his pace down the Opera House stairs. 'We can keep an eye out for your next list item while we scope out the cafes along the quay,' he said over his shoulder. 'And that chocolate shop you like, Mum. We should stop there too.'

But when they reached the bottom of the stairs, his mother pursed her lips, face turning sheepish. 'I may have already made a stop there last night after dinner with my friends, but you two go ahead,' she said. 'I might head up to the Botanical Gardens and read for a bit. I don't get much time-out back home and want to make the most of it.' She gave them a wink and started the short walk to the gardens.

Gus shrugged. 'Looks like it's just you and me,' he said. They started walking. 'I didn't mind the ballet,' he confessed a moment later.

Maya looked at him in mock astonishment.

'Don't go getting all excited. It's not like I'm gonna rush back and buy tickets for *Swan Lake*,' he said. 'But I didn't *mind* it.'

Maya dropped the mock astonished look. 'Well, if it's any consolation—' her gaze slid from his and onto the people-packed promenade ahead of them, '—I'm not about to rush back for another performance either.'

'For real?' But even as he said it, Gus could see Maya and ballet weren't exactly a duo made in dancing heaven.

'I've never been much into dance,' Maya said as they stopped so a bunch of tourists could take a photo with the Bridge and Opera House in the backdrop. 'All the prancing and jumping.'

'But your brother was?' Gus asked when they started walking again.

Maya laughed. 'No, not at all. But he fell on his prop sword for me when my grandmother gave me tickets to see *Swan Lake* for my fifteenth birthday. I'd been dropping hints about skateboards all year, but Grandma Sorenson felt I needed to balance my time under the hood of a car with something refined and cultured. Tickets to the ballet it was. I was seriously miffed and planned a boycott, until Michael talked me out of it, saying he'd come too. He sat through all four acts as Grandma Sorenson glared over the rim of her glasses at me.' Her eyes unfocused for a moment, the memory taking her to another ballet at another time.

Gus's gaze dipped to her hand as she felt for the leather cord on her wrist. 'Like Michael, I'm good with my hands, but add feet to the mix and you're in for a coordination disaster of epic proportions.'

The image of Maya pirouetting awkwardly across a stage in a pair of grease-stained overalls flashed before Gus's eyes. He did a shitty job of hiding his grin.

'Don't laugh.' Maya bumped him with her shoulder and he almost walked into a kid barrelling along the promenade in a pair of roller-skates.

'I'm not laughing.' Except he totally was. 'But I kind of figured you enjoyed the bridge climb more than the ballet.'

'What about you? What did you think of the climb?'

Gus jerked his head back, surprised at her question. 'It was great. I'd definitely buy repeat performance tickets to that. Why do you even need to ask?'

Maya shrugged. 'Just ... I don't know, you seemed a bit off at the start,' she said.

Gus slipped his hands into his pant pockets and looked out across the harbour. Just looking at the bridge brought back feelings of guilt. 'Sometimes I feel like I shouldn't get the chance to do stuff like that.'

He glanced Maya's way, found her brow furrowed with confusion.

'I mean, because other people will never get the chance,' he said, then copied Maya's frown. Looking for a distraction, he pointed to an Italian restaurant across the promenade. 'This alright with you?'

Maya nodded. The frown was gone, but now her expression was dangerously thoughtful. He should have kept his mouth shut.

They took a seat at one of the outside tables and ordered coffees with their dessert. The waiter left, and Maya smiled all casual and relaxed at him.

People piled off a ferry on the jetty opposite. Above them, in the distance, she spotted tiny dots moving across the bridge arch like ants. 'Michael would have loved this,' she said. 'Not so much the ballet, but the bridge ... he'd have loved climbing that bridge.'

And there it was again, the chainmail guilt, weighing him down, making him slide lower into his chair in a futile attempt to escape it.

'Pat would have loved climbing that bridge, too,' Gus said.

'That doesn't mean you can't enjoy it,' Maya whispered.

Gus blinked at Maya's words. He hadn't meant to admit his guilt out loud. Or maybe he had. Maybe he knew she'd argue his point. Maybe, just quietly, he wanted her to.

He peered across the small metal table at her. 'We used to talk about it, about climbing the bridge.' He pulled the bowl of sugar packets on the table closer, took one out, toyed with it to give his fingers something to do. 'Pat kept putting it off, though. Either school was too busy, or he felt he couldn't leave the farm, or whatever. Something always got in the way. And now ...' He looked up. Maya's eyes were on him, large and full of pity, and he got the feeling not all her compassion was for his brother.

'Quit looking at me like that,' he said. 'I'm not the one you need to feel sorry for.'

She raised a brow at him. 'What, and your brother is?'

Gus straightened in his seat. 'He deserves it more than me.'

'That doesn't mean he wants it.' Maya's words were challenging, unlike her expression, which was soft, almost like she knew that this conversation was forcing him out of his comfort zone.

'I met your brother barely five days ago,' she continued, 'but that's plenty long enough to know he's not the type to play the blame game.'

Gus's fingers stilled on the little packet of sugar. 'He told you about the accident?'

Maya nodded.

'Well, you're dead right, Pat has never blamed me for putting him in a wheelchair. Doesn't mean I don't blame myself.' Gus tossed the sugar packet onto the table and leaned forward. 'See, there's just no getting around the fact that I'm the reason he can't do a lot of the things he wants to do. Flowery sentiments don't help. All they do is compound the guilt, make it heavier and harder to shift into a space where I don't trip over it every time I find myself doing something I know Pat would have enjoyed.'

Mouth opening, then closing, Maya blinked at him. His little speech had stunned her. *Good.* Did she think she was the first to tell him he shouldn't feel guilty? *Hell no!* He'd heard it all before. From family. From friends. Even from complete strangers who felt the need to impart their unwanted wisdom.

It's not your fault.

You didn't make the bike roll.

You didn't crush his spine.

You didn't do this ... you didn't do that.

Fact is, he *did* pester Pat to race home across the paddocks. That little detail, no-one ever mentioned. And yet, that little detail was the splinter buried deep in his conscience, throbbing away under the surface of his everyday life.

Ugly, unshifting guilt.

Thankfully, the waiter arrived with their order. The interruption dialled the moment down from a nine to a four on the awkward scale.

When the waiter left, Gus observed Maya over the rim of his latte. She wasn't meeting his eyes. Not because she was deliberately avoiding looking at them. No, she had her thoughtful face on again. *Great.*

'My brother was the quiet type, almost like he thought he had a finite number of words and didn't want to waste them.' Maya dug her fork into the slice of caramel cheesecake on her plate, still not meeting Gus's gaze. 'So when he said something more than once, I took notice.'

Gus waited for the useless platitude.

When Maya decided to take a bite of her cheesecake instead, Gus almost rolled his eyes.

Finally, she put her fork down. 'You only have one past, but you have multiple futures. It's up to you which future you decide to travel towards.'

Gus straightened in his chair. He hadn't heard that one before, but it was still useless.

'It's not that simple,' he said, spearing his fork into his own dessert. Blueberry cheesecake, one of his favourites, but he suddenly had little appetite for it.

'I never said it would be simple.' Maya snagged Gus's gaze, forcing him to look up at her. 'I know you feel you need to do what you think Patrick can't do, but you're not giving him enough credit. He's very resourceful and motivated and with a little help could do a lot more, freeing you up to do … something other than farming.'

'It's not that simp—'

'I know it's not simple,' she cut him off, curled a strand of hair around her finger and slid it behind one ear with visible exasperation. 'But … it's possible.' She then edged her hand forward and gave his fingers a squeeze. 'It's possible, if you give it a chance, Gus.'

Gus frowned so hard the centre of his forehead started to ache. Was she right? Was it really possible? Because if it was, it could change everything.

Chapter Twenty-Five

Maya watched indecision play across Gus's face.

'How?' he eventually whispered, almost like he was too afraid to let anyone hear the flutter of hope in his voice.

'By helping him get back on a quad bike.'

Gus flinched and Maya winced, guilt for dragging up this painful part of Gus's life hitting her smack in the centre of her chest, but …

No. He has to hear this.

She shuffled her chair closer to the table, closer to him. 'I could make alterations to the quad so he can ride—'

'No.' Gus's voice was stone hard.

'Gus, you're not helping Patrick by keeping him from doing what he so clearly wants to do.'

Gus opened his mouth again. Maya held up her hand. 'I know this is hard for you but hear me out. Please.'

His nostrils flared but he kept quiet. Cake forgotten, his weary eyes fixed on her. Their intensity had Maya leaning back a little in her chair, but she couldn't back down now. Patrick was relying on her. And maybe, Gus too.

'There are two things I've learned about Patrick since arriving in Barangaroo Creek. One, he's got a much better sense of humour than you do, he's nicer and he makes better first impressions.'

'That's like three—'

'And—' Maya talked right over the top of him, '—he's desperate to be more involved on the farm. To do that, he needs to get back on the bike, literally.'

Gus dug his thumb and index finger into the corners of his eyes and breathed deeply through his nose. He wasn't shutting her out, no, this was the sight of a guy in pain. The thought of his brother getting back on the contraption that had almost killed him was causing him to hurt, badly.

Maya's stomach twisted but she kept right on. 'He wants this, Gus. You think you're protecting him, but what you're really doing is slowly killing him inside.' She brushed her fingers along his arm, needing to soften the truth of her words.

He dropped his hand from his face, glanced down at her fingers, then back up to find her eyes. Maya couldn't figure out if the deep grooves across Gus's forehead were a good sign or bad.

'If he gets hurt again, Maya, I don't … I can't …' He broke off, eyes focusing on something just past her shoulder. 'Pat on a quad … It scares me,' he said, still not looking at her.

'I get it, I do.'

Gus pushed back in his chair so suddenly the cups on the table wobbled. 'That's just it, you don't. You're not responsible for putting your brother in a wheelchair.'

Gus's words … liquid concrete pouring slowly into Maya's lungs. She grabbed her coffee cup with a shaky hand and took a gulp. But she needed to push through. She wanted to help Patrick, even if it meant showing Gus the ugly truth about her very real shortcomings.

She set her cup down and looked Gus square in the eyes. 'A bee sting might have sent my brother into anaphylaxis, but it was my incompetence that killed him.'

Gus blinked at her, features scrunched in confusion. 'What?'

'The fan belt. Michael had shown me how to replace it only days before we broke down, but I'd been distracted, worrying about that stupid history quiz that was the reason we went for a drive in the first place. I didn't pay attention, and when I went to swap the snapped fan belt for the one Michael made me keep in the boot for emergencies, I forgot to tighten the fasteners. A couple of miles down the road the whole thing came off and the engine overheated. Instead of racing towards the ambulance we'd called, I watched my brother gasp his last breath.' Maya swallowed past the bitter tasting lump in her throat. 'So don't tell me I don't know, Gus, because I do.'

Stone still, Gus stared at her. She could see the words forming on his lips. Words she'd heard countless times from countless different mouths. Words that were as much true as they were false …

'You know you can't think like that. It's not your fault,' he said.

She pinned his gaze with hers. 'Just like Patrick's accident isn't yours, right?'

He huffed, a humourless sound. He finally got it. He understood.

Maya leant forward, touched her hand to his arm again. 'Patrick has chosen which future he wants to travel towards. I can't help my brother anymore, Gus, but together we can help yours. Your fear of repeating this one part of Patrick's past is keeping him from living the future he wants.' *And you*, she wanted to add. It was keeping Gus from living the future he wanted, too.

The hope she'd heard in his voice earlier surfaced in Gus's eyes as he looked at her, even if it was rimmed with red raw panic. 'You really think … You think you can make alterations to the quad so that Pat can use it?'

Yes! She nodded, a tentative smile spreading across her face. 'I think I can.'

Gus chewed on his thumbnail, those creases across his forehead returning. 'We'd need to convince Mum and Dad, and do everything possible to keep him from falling out or rolling or—' he ran both hands over his face, '—I can't believe I'm even contemplating this.'

But Maya could believe it. Gus loved his brother. This was the right thing to do. She grabbed his hand and squeezed. 'You won't regret this, you'll see.'

He glanced at their hands on the table but didn't make any moves to remove his. It felt oddly right.

'We can run it by your parents when we get back to the farm tonight,' she said, 'and if they're good with the idea, we can get started tomorrow.'

'Let's run it by Mum on the way home in the car,' Gus said. 'If we can bring her round, then Dad should be easy.'

She could believe that. Of the three of them, Gus was always going to be the hardest to convince.

Further down from the restaurant, a far-off techno beat and low tuba-like drone caught her attention. 'Hey, is that what I think it is?' She turned to look down the promenade but couldn't see past all the people.

'Sounds like it.' Gus smiled and waved for the waiter to bring their bill.

They half-walked half-ran the stretch until they came to the overseas passenger terminal. There, a group of Indigenous musicians made one of the most hypnotic concoctions of sound Maya had ever heard. The modern techno beat strangely suited the didgeridoo's bone-deep bass notes but didn't overpower the rhythm of the clap sticks.

Gus somehow manoeuvred them to the front of the crowd so Maya could have an up-close look. Two male musicians sitting on a rug spread on the ground wore nothing more than loin cloths and tribal paint markings on their skin. The whole set up of didgeridoo and sticks and body paint was put on for overseas tourists like herself but Maya didn't mind. It was something Michael had wanted to experience. She wouldn't change a thing. She pulled out her phone to take a photo.

The song came to an end and the younger of the two musicians held out a clap stick to the audience.

'Who wants a go?'

Gus looked at her, a question in his eyes.

'Would you?' she asked.

He smiled and stepped forward.

The older guy handed him a didgeridoo. 'Give it a good blow, mate, like a trumpet,' he said, then scooped up a second pair of clap sticks and hooked into the beat.

Gus put the instrument to his lips—and blew the mother of all raspberries. Maya bit down on a grin. Gus tried again—for an even bigger raspberry blowout. Half a minute later, he'd still not produced a decent sound. He shrugged and handed the didgeridoo back to its owner.

'Thank you.' Maya bumped his shoulder with his as they turned to walk back down the promenade.

Gus raised a brow. 'For sounding like a cow with explosive diarrhoea?'

'For helping me complete Michael's list.'

His smile warmed her. 'So that's item number six off the list.'

'Yes, only one more to go.' She'd almost done it. Not even a week into her stay and she'd all but completed her brother's list.

She smiled, but the corners of her lips were heavy, a feeling of uncertainty about what came next weighing them down.

Chapter Twenty-Six

'Do you need a hand getting onto the quad?' Gus couldn't believe he was asking his brother that question. An unnecessary one, it seemed, as Pat was nearly levitating with excitement at riding a quad bike for the first time since the accident. Four years of using nothing but his upper body meant his brother lifted himself easily out of his wheelchair and onto the four-wheel bike.

The unguarded elation on Pat's face set off a dangerous prickle behind Gus's eyes. He turned to pick up Pat's helmet and give himself a moment to blink the sting away. He wished he could deal as easily with the roil of nausea in his stomach.

Before he could hand his brother the helmet, Mum took it from him and proceeded to secure it on Pat's head. 'Now, take it nice and easy this time round. Maybe up and down the drive, then straight back here. It's been a while and the wiring's different and you don't want to—'

'Mum.' Pat pulled her hands from the helmet straps and held them tight in his. 'I'll be fine.'

Gus swallowed. God, he hoped his brother was right.

Getting the message, Mum gave Pat a quick hug and stepped back to stand with Dad, who'd been watching—quietly sceptical—from the side of the shed.

His mother's response to their suggestion that Maya should alter the quad hadn't surprised Gus. Of the three of them, she'd felt Patrick's frustration the most from the start. Maybe it was motherly intuition, or maybe she just understood Pat better than Dad and Gus did. She'd even half toyed with the idea of buying a Wolverine side-by-side when Pat approached her and Dad with the idea a year after the accident. Dad had shut it down.

Gus was ashamed to admit it, but he'd been silently thankful for his father's definitive 'no'. The thought of Pat riding anything on his own grabbed him by the chest so hard his ribs ached like he'd broken each and every one of them. His father's aversion was different; he couldn't get past the conviction that, without his legs, Pat would be a hindrance rather than a help.

Well—*surprise, surprise*—Dad's attitude still hadn't changed much. Mum's resolve, however, had, and this time, she pulled out her *don't-mess-with-me* voice and argued Pat's case. Add Gus's one-eighty on his brother's wishes, as well as Pat's reminder he was no longer underage and could technically do whatever the hell he wanted, and Dad really couldn't say no. Well, he could have, but Richard Robertson wasn't anyone's fool; he knew this was one argument not worth the fight.

So, after watching Maya make the necessary alterations to Thumper for most of the day—and helping wherever he could—they were ready to test her handiwork.

'Remember, left front brake is now your rear foot brake.' Maya circled around to the front of the bike and squeezed the brake in question. 'Whatever you do, don't use the right handbrake on its own or you'll likely flip the bike.'

An 'oof' escaped Gus's mouth like someone had punched him. Beside him, Ralph pressed his muzzle into his leg. As dopey as the dog usually was, he read Gus like a farmer did the weather; he could tell a low-pressure system was coming.

Maya shot a glance over her shoulder, her gaze colliding with Gus's.

'But you'll be fine,' she rushed to add. The reassurance was for Patrick, but she was still looking at Gus.

Get a grip, for sheep's sake. He dragged shaky hands down his shorts, dug his fingers into his thighs on the way. He had to get hold of himself. This was all about Pat, not him. It was time. He *needed* to get a grip.

Pat turned the key in the quad's ignition. The bike roared to life and sent Gus's gut lurching.

Grip. Get it. Now!

His brother took a deep breath, let it out on a shaky exhale—excitement wasn't the only emotion coursing through the guy's veins.

'Here we go,' Pat said, and the bike inched forward. Slowly at first, then faster. Almost as fast as the blood rushing in Gus's ears.

'Go easy!' Mum ran out of the shed after Pat. No use, the quad was already out of earshot, snaking its way up the long drive.

With his brother on it.

Gus squeezed his eyes shut, opened them, clenched his fists. His fingernails dug into his palms, knife-like, sharp. The pain helped chase away the horrifying images his brain pushed on him and he zeroed in on Pat zooming up the dirt road drive.

Safe. Unharmed. With Ralph yapping behind him, little legs powering like his next meal depended on it. *Traitor of a dog.*

'He's doing great.' Maya's voice broke through the deafening whoosh of dread still ringing in Gus's ears. A squeeze of her hand on his arm dragged his eyes away from Pat's disappearing back to her face.

'He's going to be fine,' she said, fingers tightening again, emphasising her words. 'You need to let go.'

Gus nodded. She was right. He needed to let go. Of the guilt. Of the fear. Of the hold these two had on both Pat's and his life. Knowing she was right didn't make the letting go any easier, though.

'He's coming back!' Mum bounced a little on the spot, the grin on her face almost as wide as Pat's. 'He's got the hang of it, Richard. He's really got the hang of it.' She grabbed onto her hat with both hands. Her excitement pulled one of Gus's smiles out of hiding.

'All fine and good on the driveway,' his father said, 'but the real test will be out in the paddocks.'

That'd be right, the old man just couldn't let Pat have his moment. Still, despite all the grumbling, there was no mistaking the way his father's chest expanded and … Wait, was that a glimmer of pride in the hardened farmer's eyes?

Pat pulled the quad bike to a stop in front of the shed, the putter of the four-wheeler the only sound for a moment.

Until Pat let out a massive *whoop*.

His face beamed. There was no other way to describe it. His brother's expression was lit like a bushfire.

'This is so freaking awesome!' His smiling eyes landed first on Mum, who ran over to him before he'd even finished his outburst, and gathered him in a hug.

Over Mum's shoulder, Pat briefly glanced at Dad before fixing his gaze on Maya.

'Thank you,' he said, voice thickening with emotion.

Hands in her back pockets, Maya rocked back on her heels, her smile bigger than Gus had ever seen it. 'You're welcome.'

Mum finally pulled away and let the poor guy breathe. That's when he looked over at Gus. Pat's nod was brief, but Gus recognised it for the silent 'thank you' that it was.

His throat closed over, the significance of the moment suddenly clear and so weighty it nailed him to the dry earth under his feet. What had he been thinking? What had given him the right to keep his brother from living? He'd been pushing Pat back into his wheelchair every time he tried a way to lift himself out.

Somehow, Gus forced his body into motion and stepped up to his brother on the quad bike. 'So, next up, the paddocks. I'll take the ute out with you tomorrow.' He shoved his hands into his shorts pockets and ran his eyes over the dust-red tires of the bike, the handles vibrating gently under his brother's hands—anywhere but

Pat's eyes in case he found the rejection he deserved reflected there. 'If you want, that is,' he added quietly.

'Yeah, I want,' he said, tugging Gus's cap over his eyes. Probably to lighten the suddenly awkward moment—the Robertsons had always sucked at showing emotions.

When Gus pulled his cap back into place, he found Pat considering him. 'Any reason we can't head out to the paddocks today?'

Other than delaying seeing his brother ride a quad bike along the same stretch that almost killed him just that little bit longer? Yeah, Gus had a legitimate reason not to take Pat out there today.

'Maya has one more item on her list,' Gus said, looking over to where his mother had joined Maya and his father at the entrance to the shed. 'Sleep out under the Southern Cross.'

'Ah, I see.'

Gus whipped his head back around, eyes narrowing at the raised eyebrow in his brother's voice. 'What's that supposed to mean?'

Pat shrugged. 'If I had the choice, I'd rather be sleeping out under the Southern Cross with a cute mechanic instead of paddock bashing with my brother, too.'

Gus peered over his shoulder at Maya in her denim shorts and *Mr Men* T-shirt, trying to explain to his mother what it was that she'd done to Pat's bike.

'It has nothing to do with her being cute,' he said. *A good mechanic? Sure. Determined and savvy? Hell yeah. Intuitive and, well, kind? Definitely. But cute?*

She caught him looking and frowned. No surprise, since his own expression was likely all squished-up and suspicious as he gawked at her. Quickly, his eyes found the ground and Ralph's brown-and-white back as the dog sniffed the wheels of the quad bike.

'Better get this quad into the shed.' He tapped Thumper's wheel with his foot and pulled his cap lower to hide the sudden flash of heat stealing its way across his face. Because damn if his brother wasn't right—he was about to sleep under the stars with a cute mechanic.

Chapter Twenty-Seven

The heat of the day had dialled down from unbearable to slightly unbearable by the time Maya and Gus made their way up a bush-covered mountain. Okay, maybe not a mountain. More like a big hill, really.

The vegetation was both dense and sparse somehow up here. The dirt road they travelled along was lined with gum tree after gum tree, and other spindly bushes and shrubs Maya didn't know the names of. Green stretched as far as the eye could see, but it was a washed-out, sun-scorched yellowy-brown-green, not the deep and heavy green of back home. Splashes of colour between the trees were rare, the odd dry and faded yellow banksia—Jen had taught her the name—was the only flower that whizzed past the pick-up's window on a regular basis as they wound their way up towards …

Maya turned to look at Gus. 'Where are we going again?'

'To sleep under the Southern Cross,' Gus told her, not taking his eyes from the windy fire trail.

She sighed. 'I know that.' He'd said as much after they'd helped Patrick stash the quad bike back in the shed. 'I mean where *exactly* are we going.'

'Mount Frae waterhole.' Gus twitched his eyebrows in her direction like she was meant to be impressed with this information.

'Only the locals know about it, and cause it's on private land—technically, the McGowans own this peak and the surrounding bushland—we're not likely to run into any bushwalkers. The odd kangaroo, maybe, but other than that we'll have the Southern Cross all to ourselves.'

'A waterhole? Around here?' She swept a hand along the windscreen and the sunstroke-affected vegetation beyond it. 'You said yourself this place hasn't seen any decent rain in months.' She'd gotten excited when he'd told her to pack swimwear. Excitement now turned to scepticism.

Gus tsked. 'Have a bit of faith. This waterhole is a natural spring and I haven't ever seen it dry up completely, at least not in the eighteen years I've been coming up here.' He turned her way, eyes dancing in the light of the late afternoon sun. 'It might not be brimming but it'll be full enough for you to have a less touristy swimming experience than Bondi Beach and its budgie-smuggler lifeguards.'

'Budgie what?'

'Budgie smugglers. Swimmers guys wear that show—' he rolled his eyes and shook his head. 'Never mind. The point is, it's an awesome place to cool off and lie under the stars, trust me.'

Trust him. She didn't have much choice. It was only the two of them heading up to this mysterious—probably snake and lizard infested—waterhole, so it was just as well she trusted him. Suddenly the truth of that hit her. Maya sat up a little straighter in the passenger seat; she trusted him, trusted Gus. Maybe it was their truce, or the weekend in Sydney, or possibly his turnaround on Patrick and the quad bike, but at some recent point she'd stopped seeing him as the uptight outback cowboy and started seeing him as Gus, the possible friend.

She took in his profile as he navigated the pick-up around a tricky corner. The Southern Cross was the last of the dot points on her list. What did that mean for the rest of her stay? Would he now consider his host job done and leave her to her own devices for the next five weeks? The prospect dragged down the corners of her mouth and hollowed out her belly. She didn't want this newfound truce-come-friendship between them to end, not when she was only now starting to enjoy his company.

Just short of two hours after they'd left the farm, Gus turned the pick-up onto a dirt path off the fire trail. Branches scraped the car in a knife-down-a-porcelain-plate squeal as Gus coaxed it along the narrow, barely-there track.

Just when she thought he'd gotten them lost, the track spat them out in a small clearing.

'Here we are,' Gus said and stopped the pick-up a few yards from the edge of a large natural pool. 'Behold the Mount Frae waterhole.' He peered across at her, mouth twisting in a wry smile. 'What do you think?'

Fairy grotto. There was no other way to describe it. *Bush fairies had to live here!* Hugged by a four-or-so-yard-high rock ledge on the far end, the crisp green-blue pool shimmered invitingly in the remnant rays of the sun. Tall gum trees stood guard in a tight circle all around, protecting and hiding the swimming hole. No wonder Gus and the locals kept this little cool watery heaven a secret.

'Wow,' Maya eventually said.

'Right?' Gus hopped out of the pick-up, grabbing their backpacks and sleeping bags from the back tray. He dropped them on a cleared bit of ground that looked like it had already hosted a sleeping bag or two in the past, while Maya took a closer look at the waterhole. The water was clear and clean up close, its green-blue tinge a reflection of the overhanging shrubs and bushes. She could see right to the bottom of the pool, the edge of which was lined with smooth rocks and mossy boulders and—

'Are those tadpoles?' She pointed at the thumbnail-sized black wrigglers on one of the flatter rocks in the shallow water near the pool's edge.

Gus grinned. 'Yep. Made sure there were some up here especially, so you'd feel at home and all.'

Maya shoved his shoulder. Unfortunately, the guy had decent balance and didn't end up face first in the water like she'd hoped.

'Okay, okay.' Gus held up his hands in apology. 'Too soon, I get it, but you're not going to let a few tadpoles keep you from enjoying a dip, are you?' He eyed her as he pulled off his shoes.

Maya cast her gaze over the inviting water, the sky's warm ochre bleeding into the cool of the pool. She reached for her own shoes, tugged them off and straightened up to a sight almost as Instagram-worthy as the fairy grotto.

Gus Robertson without his shirt on.

Between swim classes and show-pony-jocks doing their track and field workouts, she'd seen her fair share of pecs on parade at school. But Gus's was definitely worth a second—and maybe third—gawk.

She'd discovered that Thursday night, just after *he'd* discovered the huntsman in his underwear drawer. She'd been careful to mask her appreciation then. They'd been on opposite sides of an unspoken war. At the time the last thing Maya needed was to give Gus ammunition that she thought he was ... that she found him ... that ... damn, the guy was built.

But that's not why you like him. The realisation rushed at her out of nowhere and, hands on the hem of her T-shirt, she paused just as she was about to pull it over her head.

'You forgot your swimmers, didn't you?' Gus frowned, eyes dipping to her hands gripping her top, then back up to her face again.

'No, all good.'

Maya tugged the tank over her head and made quick work of her shorts. She wore the same bikini tank top and bottoms she'd worn to the beach in Sydney. But out here, she and Gus were the only people around, whereas on Bondi beach they'd been surrounded by crowds of hundreds. She felt strangely self-conscious.

Gus didn't seem to have the same problem. If he did, he hid it well, because other than giving her a quick once over, he nodded like he was satisfied with her choice of outfit, and waded into the water. Maya shrugged and followed him in.

She took careful steps across the slippery flat boulders near the edge, then found silt with her feet and allowed herself to relax, skimming her hands across the surface of the cool silky water until it was deep enough for her to swim a few strokes.

'Do you come up here often?' she asked, swimming up to Gus where he was floating on his back in the middle of the pool.

'Not often enough,' he said, eyes on the violet pre-twilight sky, hands moving gently back and forth next to him in the water. 'We used to come up here all the time. End of shearing season we'd goof off in the pool then sit around a camp fire, stuffing our faces with whatever we'd managed to pilfer from the pantry.'

Eyes to the sky and hands back and forth, Maya lay on her back and mirrored his actions. 'You and Patrick, you mean?'

'Yeah, Pat and me and Ruth and whoever was around.' The movement of his hands in the water slowed. 'Now I trek up here alone, when I need some time-out or to think.'

'Or to help an annoying house guest tick off the last item on her clichéd must-do list?'

'Or that,' Gus said, the smile loud and clear in his tone.

Suddenly, Gus disappeared under the surface of the water and reappeared further along the pool, hair slick and dripping dark into his eyes. 'I kinda don't mind this list item.' He flicked water at Maya and grinned.

She wiped water from her eyes. 'And why's that?' she asked, splashing him right back.

He dove below the surface and she lost him in the moving shadows cast by the dipping sun and looming trees.

A moment later, his voice came from behind her, 'Cause it means I can do …'

She spun in the water and her gaze snagged on the warning glint in his eyes.

'This!'

The next second the world tilted and she gasped at the darkening sky before the water swallowed her yelp as she went under. She bobbed up to the surface, splashing and spluttering, but found no remorse in Gus's expression.

'Think that's funny, huh?' She brushed tangles of sopping hair from her eyes even as she inched towards him through the water.

'Hell yeah!' But he must have guessed what was coming because he backed away from her.

Not fast enough, Farmer Boy.

Maya launched herself at his shoulders and unbalanced him enough to dunk his head under water. She meant business.

There were squeals and laughter and splashes and lunacy, until they heaved their exhausted bodies out of the pool and collapsed onto their towels. Once again, a truce drawn.

Chapter Twenty-Eight

Gus was happy just to lie there and watch day dip into night, his skin drying in the warm evening breeze. His breath slowed to the backdrop of buzzing cicadas.

'I should get Pat up here again.'

'You should,' Maya said.

'We could muck around in the water like we used to, sit by the fire ... talk.'

'I think he'd like that,' Maya said, nodding.

'And to listen to him,' he added. 'I should have listened to him way before this.' Gus shifted on his towel and turned to face her. 'The look on his face when he pulled up on that quad ...' He shook his head, unable to contain the smile splitting his face. 'I may never have seen that look if it weren't for you. I'd have kept on listening to all the fears I had about Pat getting hurt again instead of listening to him, hearing what he wanted, what he needed. That was your doing, so ... thank you.'

His words sent a flush over her cheeks. It made him smile all the more.

'No need to thank me,' she whispered. 'I'm sure you would have heard him eventually.'

'Maybe.' But it may have been too late by then.

'So, now that you've listened to your brother ...' Maya paused and eyed him for a silent second, '... any chance you might listen to yourself?'

Gus narrowed his eyes at her. 'What do you mean?' he said. Although he knew exactly what she meant.

'Now that he's more mobile, Pat can be more hands-on around the farm, which means you might be able to—'

Gus snorted. 'It doesn't work that way. Even if Pat ends up helping more—and that's a big *if*—I'm still expected to contribute. This farm—this life—it's where I'm expected to be, what I'm expected to do.' Gus raked a hand over the ground. A swift flick of his wrist and the palm-sized pebble he'd picked up, all jagged like his patience, landed in the water with a *plomp*.

Beside him, Maya shifted on her towel. She was watching him, thinking. He felt the scrutiny of her eyes on his profile while he stared up into the near-dark sky.

'Would it hurt to tell your father the truth?' she eventually asked.

Would it ever. 'You've met my father, Maya. How do you think he'd react if I tapped him on the shoulder and told him I didn't want to do this farming gig? That what I *really* wanted to do was play with non-existent computer-generated creatures instead of looking after the animals that've paid for my entire livelihood.'

That'd go down about as well as a lamb roast without gravy.

Another stone hit the water with a *plomp*. Bigger this time.

She turned on her side. 'You make it sound like you're some spoilt, self-indulgent kid running from his responsibilities.' Her breath brushed his face as she spoke.

Gus resumed a steady rhythm of *scrape, throw, plomp. Scrape, throw, plomp*. He wanted to believe her. He so badly wanted to believe her, but ...

When he turned Maya's way, the whites of her eyes were bright and hopeful in the scraps of evening light as he looked at her, and it killed him a little to disappoint her. 'I don't think it's a good idea to say anything.'

Maya opened her mouth but Gus turned away again, profile pointing to the sky. 'Not yet anyway,' he added. 'It's too early. Dad needs some time to get used to the changes with Pat first. If I say something now it'll be too much too soon.'

Maya edged forward. 'Does that mean you'll say something eventually though?'

Would he? Did he have the strength to finally tell his parents his dreams didn't align with theirs? Could he face the fallout? Because if there was one thing he was sure of it was that there would be a fallout.

He gripped a nearby rock and squeezed, pushed the jagged edges in to his palm. 'A month,' he said. 'I'll give Dad a month to adjust to Pat being more active, more involved. Then I'll plant the idea of Pat maybe one day ... doing even more, and me ... doing something else.' Gus shifted on his towel. The ground was hard, but saying those words, making that promise to Maya—and himself—was the real source of his discomfort. Time to change the direction of this discussion.

'Tell me about Michael's diary.' He turned to face her again. 'What did the last entry you read say?'

Chapter Twenty-Nine

Maya knew exactly what Gus was doing. Normally she would have deflected his subtle-as-a-brick attempt to change the subject, but she found she wanted to talk to him about Michael.

'I only found the diary four months ago.' When she'd braved going into his room for the first time since his death. 'It's this plain ring-bound notebook. Blank pages, no lines, with a bit of leather cord keeping it all bound up tight.' Maya brushed her wrist, the leather there still damp.

'So if you're reading one entry per week, that means you've read …'

'Sixteen. I've read up to January sixteenth.'

'And? What was it about?'

'Antifreeze.'

'Antifreeze? For real?'

Maya smiled. 'Yep, Michael had shown me how to flush a radiator that day and told me this story about some little old granny in Wyoming, who'd knocked off members of her family one by one with antifreeze in her homemade lemonade.' She flopped back onto her towel and brushed her hand along the dirt, feeling for her own rock to throw. 'His diary entry for the day was all about the irony that something so toxic was so delicious, rounded off by a few tips on how to use antifreeze effectively … in *mechanics* not murders, of course.'

'Intellectual as well as practical,' Gus said. 'I think I might have liked your brother.'

Maya grinned. 'I think you might have, too. He was a tragic car geek, but he was also patient and encouraging, and he really was a magician when it came to fixing cars.'

'So is that what you'll do when you get home? Work alongside your dad in the garage like Michael did?'

Thankfully, they were both staring at the darkening purple promise of the sky; that way Gus couldn't see the colour slide off Maya's face at his question.

'I've been accepted at Wheaton. I start as soon as I get back.' Maya pitched her rock into the darkness. The *plomp* when it hit the water was a piddly letdown.

'To study what?'

'Don't know yet. I won't need to decide on a major for a couple of years so …' Maya shrugged. She hadn't really thought about what she'd focus on other than the list.

Gus stirred beside her until she felt his eyes on her profile. 'I don't get it. From what I've seen, you love working with cars as much as your brother did, so why wouldn't you …' he propped himself up on one arm, '… I've got it, your parents want you to go to college, is that it?'

'No, that's my decision.' She felt for another rock to hurl into the void.

Gus stared at her through the darkness. 'That's ironic.'

She turned his way with a frown. 'How?'

'Well, here I am, forced into my brother's badly fitting shoes, while you're avoiding Michael's perfectly fitting ones.'

Maya stilled. It was dark. It wasn't fair that Gus saw things so clearly. But there were some things he had no way of seeing, like the fear of falling short in Michael's shadow that Maya carried around inside.

'You might not want to run the farm for your brother, but you're more than capable of doing it. Me, on the other hand …' She looped two fingers through the leather cord around her wrist to remind her what it was that kept her back. 'Michael was an exceptional mechanic. I'll never be able to replace him.'

'You don't have to replace him.' Gus edged closer. 'I've seen what you can do. You just have to be you,' he said, squeezing her hand.

Maya squeezed his fingers back, then pulled them out of his hand. 'It's not that simple.'

When he didn't say anything, she looked up to find the white flash of his teeth. 'It might not be simple,' he said, 'but it's possible … if you give it a chance.'

Maya fought her smile but lost. Turning her own words against her was such a Michael thing to do. Gus was right; the two of them would have got along real fine.

Suddenly, Maya was aware of how much the space between them had shrunk. How she could barely hear the buzz of the cicadas over the quickening military tattoo of her heart. How her skin tingled in the shadow of his touch.

They leant in at the same time, lips brushing gently, first this way, then that. He tasted of summer, of surprises all sweet and scary and unexpected.

And amusement, apparently, because his mouth was grinning against hers.

Maya pulled back. 'What's so funny?'

Still smiling, he traced warm fingers over her arm. 'I came out here to show you the Southern Cross, and here I am the one seeing stars.'

Maya spluttered a laugh. 'Seriously? That's the corniest line I've ever heard.' It wasn't just corny, it was downright … 'Clichéd! Ha!' She poked him in the chest. 'You know what you just did? You served me a clichéd line.'

He cringed and looked away and—hold up one minute!—was that a flush stealing across his cheekbones? She couldn't be sure—the sun had now fully disappeared—but she could have sworn the guy was blushing.

'I'll let you get away with it if you finally show me this elusive Southern Cross,' she said.

'Easy,' he whispered into her hair and pointed to five bright stars in the shape of a cross in the ocean of dots above them.

Maya smiled; her list was complete.

'Thank you,' she said, taking in the sight above her.

'You're welcome,' Gus whispered beside her.

They lay there and breathed in the stars. *I hope you're watching,* she thought to the sky.

'What am I going to do for the rest of my stay now that my list is all ticked off?' Maya said after a while.

'Again, easy. I'll help you make a new must-do list. Give you a taste of what the locals have to offer.'

'No snakes though, right?'

Gus scratched his chin, pretending to think. 'Can't guarantee that, sorry,' he said, not looking one bit apologetic.

Head cocked and narrowed, eyes taking his measure, Maya said, 'So you like sleeping with huntsmen, do you?'

She felt a shudder roll through him and grinned.

'Fine, no snakes!' Gus said quickly. 'Guess we'll have to add something else to the list instead.'

'What did you have in mind?'

'Want me to show you?' he asked, pulling her closer.

Maya nodded. This time it was her turn to grin against his lips.

Chapter Thirty

The next morning Gus woke to the cracking duet of local whipbirds. He stretched, arms slipping free of his sleeping bag, muscles protesting a night spent on the uneven ground, and took in the sun's position on the crisp sheet of blue morning sky.

Around seven, he guessed. Not often he got to sleep in this late, but no surprise, really. It had been late when he and Maya finally crawled into their sleeping bags after their tinned spaghetti dinner and bag-of-jellybeans dessert. Even then they'd talked into the early morning. And in between all the talking …

Snatches of the night flashed in Gus's mind and his face warmed. He peered over at Maya, tucked snuggly into her sleeping bag still sound asleep. This time of year, the nights were far from cold, but he'd made sure he'd retreated to the safety zone of his sleeping bag. He didn't want Maya to feel in any way uncomfortable about spending the night out camping with him, and zipping himself up in his sleeping bag seemed like the best way to let her know that.

She must have followed suit because all he saw peeking out the top of her sleeping bag was an out-of-control mop of black hair framing her sleeping, slightly flushed, face. He allowed himself a closer look. Not too long, though—*watching people sleep is creepy*—just long enough to appreciate the relaxed curl of her full bottom lip, the soft fan of her lashes over her cheeks.

He snorted and she stirred but didn't wake. The irony; him ending up liking the very girl who kept him from doing what he loved these holidays. He might be missing out on the CGI course this summer, but if it hadn't been for Maya landing in his sheep paddock, he could be missing out on seeing his brother's renewed lease on country life.

He let her sleep and got up to use the *bush bathroom*, then rummaged through his backpack for the muesli bars he'd packed for their breakfast. Not the most appealing of breakfast options, especially without a cup of coffee to help the processed oats go down. As for the coffee, they'd have to wait until they made it back into town. There was a full fire ban in place, so no way for them to boil water. Gus didn't mind. He'd never liked drinking the sweetened dishwater dross that was instant coffee.

A nearby rock made a good spot to chew away on his muesli bar and check his phone while he waited for Maya to wake up. Reception up here wasn't the best but he found the usual slew of social media messages, a few new likes on the latest special effects video he'd uploaded the other night, and a couple of missed calls.

Both from Mum.

One last night and another one this morning.

He scratched his chin; he couldn't remember the mobile ringing, but then he'd been a bit distracted.

There was a voicemail. Thanks to the dodgy reception, the recorded message was scratchy at best, but he made out the important bits: *Dad and Pat ... in the paddocks ... the quad ... accident ... up at the hospital ... call me.*

The mouthful of muesli bar suddenly dry and sticky in his throat, he pressed *return call*. The mobile only rang twice before three beeps told him he was out of range. He slapped the useless phone against his thigh. *Shitty country network.* An image of Pat lying bruised and broken under the quad bike flooded his brain. For a moment he couldn't move; dread locking his limbs and stabbing his chest.

Suddenly, he stood, the urgency of the situation jump-starting his body.

'Maya!' He shook her by the shoulder. 'Wake up.' The sooner they got off this mountain the better. He needed to get to the hospital and fast.

She stirred, eyes blinking against the glare of the morning sun. 'What time is it?'

'Time to go.' He shoved his sleeping bag into his backpack without bothering to roll it up. 'There's been an accident. Pat's in hospital.'

That bit of news had her scrambling up. 'What? How?' Her face lost some of its previous flush as she quickly started collecting her stuff.

'Don't know for sure.' Mum's message had been too cryptic. 'He must have convinced Dad to take him out on the quad again after we left.' Bloody impatient, his brother was. Although, a small part of Gus was thankful it hadn't been him out with Pat when the accident had happened. Watching his brother come off the bike a second time would have … Gus shook his head to clear the paralysing image from his mind. He couldn't go there. Not again. Not when it could all have been avoided.

Pat should never have got on that quad bike.

Anger rushed him like a charging ram. He slapped his backpack onto the tray of the ute.

'I can't get hold of Mum. No reception up here. I need to get to the hospital,' he snapped, then pinched his eyes shut. *Crap.* Maya didn't deserve the raw end of his mood. *Or did she?*

His eyes flew open, gaze flicking over to find Maya's. Her brows dipped, lips pressing tight like she'd heard his unspoken question. She didn't say anything, just placed her backpack—gently—next to his and climbed into the passenger seat.

Chapter Thirty-One

'Are you upset with me?' The tension in the car forced Maya to acknowledge the question.

'Why would I be upset with you?' He didn't look at her. Not even a glance. And she didn't miss how his hands tightened around the steering wheel.

'Because of my part in all this.'

'Your part?'

If the situation had been any less serious, she would have rolled her eyes at him. Of course he knew her part in this. The way he'd looked at her before they'd climbed into the ute had been all about her part in this.

She turned in her seat so she could see his expression when she asked the question that'd been forming, thick and bitter, on her tongue. 'You think this is my fault, don't you?' She watched him, eyes narrowed.

She deserved the truth, even if it hurt. And by the tight line of Gus's jaw, it was going to.

'You weren't there,' he said, still not looking at her.

This time she did roll her eyes. 'Maybe, but I amended the quad bike. I made it possible.'

His jaw clamped tighter, like he was trying to hold back what he really wanted to say. She waited, eyes tracking the bob of his Adam's Apple against the backdrop of shrubs and bushes whipping past them.

'You amended the quad bike, yes. You made it possible, yes.' His knuckles whitened as his fingers tightened even more around the steering wheel.

He was blaming her without saying the words.

She crossed her arms. 'Which means what, exactly?'

Say it, Gus. Just say it's my fault.

He flicked her one small glance, then his features hardened, his jaw so tight Maya was waiting to hear it crack. 'If you hadn't fiddled with the quad bike there would be no accident. That's what it means.'

Cold fingers of guilt grabbed at her shoulders, liquefying her bones and pulling her back further into the seat leather. *If you hadn't fiddled with the quad bike* ... She wanted to disappear. The truth was painful, but Gus was right; if she hadn't amended the bike there would be no accident. Pat would be safe.

And miserable.

The errant thought jolted her out of her guilt spiral. She'd only done what Patrick had asked her to. It wasn't like she'd put a gun to his head and forced him on the amended bike. He'd *wanted* this.

She gripped her seatbelt, tugged it away from her body and took a deep breath.

'You're right. If I hadn't made the changes to the quad bike everything would have gone on as before. You wouldn't be worried about losing your brother, because he'd be in his wheelchair, where he's been for the past four years, safe and sound.' She turned her unsmiling face Gus's way. 'Feeling frustrated. And resentful. And incomplete. And—'

'Stop!'

'Why?'

'Because you don't know that! You don't *know* what Pat feels.'

'But you do, don't you?'

171

Gus glared at her, eyes wide and wild but didn't say anything.

But he knew. She saw it in his panicked eyes. Buried deep under all their father's shattered expectations he *knew* the frustration Pat felt at not having more autonomy over the farm and his life. Admitting he knew, however, would have meant Patrick might have asked him for help to do something about it. And that would have meant seeing his brother back on farm machinery … and a quad bike—the stuff Gus's nightmares were made of.

Gus took the next corner too quickly. The ute swerved and groaned. Maya grabbed hold of her seatbelt to stop her shoulder smacking into the car door. Thankfully, he managed to get control before they ended up grille first in the nearest scrub.

He threw her a look like the near miss with the ditch was somehow her fault.

Was she now to blame for everything that went wrong in the guy's life?

Once they were on a straight stretch of fire trail again, he finally responded. 'I know how badly Pat wanted to get back on a quad bike—what being able to do something like that means to him—but sometimes what we want isn't what's best for us,' he said, jaw clamped tight and eyes glued to the windscreen. 'Because sometimes the risk is just not worth it, no matter how badly we want it.'

Maya narrowed her eyes at Gus's words. The words themselves were no surprise, almost predictable, the way they echoed his fear of his brother getting hurt again, maybe even his fear of letting down his father when he finally found out Gus never wanted to run the farm. But there was something else hanging on the end of his words, another—different—fear hiding between them.

… *the risk is just not worth it. No matter how badly we want it.*

'I get that you're scared for your brother, but you don't even know what's happened.'

'For all I know Pat's lying in a coma because he got on that stupid quad bike.'

'Or he's just scratched his arm on a rusty nail and needs a tetanus booster.'

Gus gave a dismissive snort and the cabin grew treacle-thick with tension again, but Maya spotted the nervous twitch in his tightly clamped jaw. There was more going on here, she just didn't know what.

'What are you really afraid of, Gus?'

In answer, he sent her a scrunched-forehead-flared-nostril glare. A quick one, but long enough to prove she'd touched a raw nerve somewhere. And long enough for Gus to completely miss seeing the—

'Kangaroo!' she yelled, pointing at the windscreen. The pick-up lurched to the right, pitching Maya shoulder first into the car door as, through the windscreen, the dusty fire trail suddenly turned into fast approaching washed-out green.

Chapter Thirty-Two

Gus slammed his foot on the brakes. There was a wail for two piercing metal-on-metal seconds, but ... Too late. The ute ploughed into a thick banksia bush, raining twigs and leaves onto the bonnet and windscreen, and sending a wave of cutting pain across his torso from shoulder to hip.

The car groaned as it settled back on its steely haunches, the side mirror dangling outside the driver side window like a two-dollar shop trinket. Steam spat from under the hood in a worrying hiss. The only thing missing was the sight of the j-walking kangaroo bouncing past them, a *you-stupid-idiot* expression on its smug face.

But the little hopper was long gone, leaving him and Maya to deal with the mess he'd left behind.

'You alright?' Placing a hand on her arm, he ran a careful eye over her. She looked a bit shell-shocked but otherwise everything else seemed to be intact.

Maya eased away the seatbelt from where it dug into her neck and rubbed her fingers along the forming welt. 'I'm fine, I think. You?'

Gus took a deep breath, felt his ribs protest but not enough to make him think there was any real damage. 'The only thing hurting at the moment is my pride.' He'd known this road was tricky. Add the very real chance of roos and … He should have paid better attention.

He unbuckled his seatbelt and eased himself out. 'Better check on the ute.'

Maya followed him out and came to stand next to him in the dirt to inspect the carnage. The roo bar had saved the ute from a trip to the panel beaters, but it'd done bugger all to stop one of the banksia branches from spearing straight through the front grille.

'Radiator would be my guess,' Maya said quietly.

His guess, too. The ute was hissing louder than an overboiled kettle. He popped the bonnet and copped a faceful of steam, which sent his own thermostat that little bit higher. *Keep it together.* He needed a clear head. He needed to get to the hospital. He needed to find out if Pat was going to be alright.

Maya peered around him. 'I could take a look …'

He shrugged and stepped aside. His roadside knowhow went as far as checking the oil gauge and changing a tyre. Maya was the grease guru, so if anyone's handiwork could get them out of this mess, it was hers.

Shame it was her handiwork that got us in this mess in the first place.

Gus ground his teeth at the thought. Playing the blame game right now wouldn't get them out of here any quicker.

He crossed his arms and stood back to let her do her thing. The growing number of lines between her brows as she peered into the bowels of his ute was dashing any hopes he had for a quick fix.

When she looked up, the bad news was written all over her face. 'The branch pierced the radiator. Not a huge crack, but it's leaked half the coolant already.' She pointed to a patch of dark green liquid pooling in the dirt. 'We'll make it a few miles before the engine overheats.'

'What if we top it up with coolant as we go?' He had a third of a canister on the tray.

Maya chewed the corner of her bottom lip. 'It might buy us a few more miles at the most.'

'Please tell me you can fix this somehow.' His voice came out strained, desperate, which was a good gauge of where he was at right about now.

'Unless you happen to have a bottle of leak sealant somewhere in the car …' She shook her head.

The only things in the car were empty soft drink bottles and chip packets along with two dozen eggs Mum had asked him to drop off at the Harrison's on their way back.

He swore under his breath, pulled his phone out and checked the number of bars. Still no reception.

He held up his phone to Maya. 'Any signal on yours?'

She pulled her mobile from her pocket and shook her head.

His fingers found the corners of his eyes and dug in. Usually the isolation of the waterhole was what made it appealing. Today not so much. They'd be lucky if anyone came past here all day. Which meant they'd have to hike until they got reception or wait until Mum and Dad realised something had gone wrong and came out here looking for them. And considering his parents had a different emergency on their mind, that could take them a while.

Gus kicked the ute's tyre. *Stupid bloody mess.*

Maya wrapped her arms around herself. 'I'm sorry.'

'Yeah, so am I.' Gus shoved the mobile into his back pocket and made his way around to the ute tray. 'Sorry you ever fixed that quad bike,' he mumbled as he pulled his water bottle from his backpack.

Behind him, Maya stopped short in the dirt. He mustn't have mumbled quietly enough.

'So you *do* think this is my fault.' Her whispered words were a complete contrast to the thunderclap in her expression.

The sun punched down on his already heated face as he chugged a long gulp of water and washed down Maya's comment. Another stinker of a day was brewing and they were stuck here, by the side of a deserted road, while his brother lay in emergency and his parents paved the worn hospital lino, hoping for the best, fearing the worst. And it could all have been avoided if—

'Yeah.' The word came out louder than he'd intended and sent Maya's eyes widening. 'Too right, this is your fault. You and your bloody fix-it attitude. Well, we've got a saying in this corner of the world: If it ain't broke, *don't* fix it. Because we were fine before you came. Perfectly fine, and then you go and stick your nose where it don't belong and Pat lands back in hospital and I can't go to my summer school and everything has gone to shit.' He hadn't moved, hadn't taken a step, but he was well aware he'd crossed a line and gone to an ugly place. It felt good, though, the heated words tumbling the weight off his shoulders.

And it felt totally shit—because deep down he didn't believe what he was saying.

But fear was a no-filter, tantrum-chucking toddler.

'Don't hold back now,' Maya said. She didn't crumble, didn't so much as step back from his barrage of accusation. The only hint that his rant had any sort of impact was a slight tremble of her hands as she crossed her arms and narrowed fiery eyes at him. 'And if it ain't broke, then why are you moping about having to take over the farm? Why are you telling your parents and Patrick lies about a surfing holiday instead of the truth?' She stuck her chin out, maybe in defiance, maybe waiting for an answer.

Well, she wasn't getting one.

Gus jammed the cap back on the water bottle and turned towards the fire trail. He needed some space. Away from the ute, from Maya, but she wouldn't take the hint.

'I'll tell you why.' Her voice was a whip crack at his shoulder. 'Because it *is* broke, but you're too much of a coward to fix it.'

Gus ground to a stop in the dirt, heard Maya's sharp intake of breath at his back as she narrowly avoided running into him.

'Coward?' He swivelled to face her. 'You're calling *me* a coward?'

'Yeah, that's exactly what I'm calling you.' She took a step closer, got right up in his face. 'You've finally got the chance to do what you love, and instead of grabbing it with both hands and fighting to make it happen you cave at the first hurdle. So yeah,' her hot, angry breath hit his face, 'you're a coward.'

A bolt of anger snapped Gus's head back. 'What about you? You think completing your stupid list will somehow bring your brother back? Whack an extra set of brakes on a quad bike and, *poof*—' Gus snapped his fingers, '—just like that you think all of Pat's and my problems are meant to be fixed?' He shook his head, mouth twisting into a snarl. 'Don't you get it? Life's not that simple. If it was, you'd be fixing your own problems. You'd be making plans to start an apprenticeship, to work with your dad in his workshop, to do what *you* love. But no, you're not doing that, are you?' He waited, gave her a chance to answer. She didn't. He knew she wouldn't. 'Who's the real coward here, Maya?'

She stood there, eyes wide, mouth agape. Frozen. Was she even breathing? A sudden stab of guilt nudged him back a step to give her some space.

She was happy to dish out her truth to him, so she better be ready when she was served a dose of his.

'Coming here was a mistake.' Maya also took a step back. 'I never wanted to be here, and you sure as heck never wanted me here.' Another step back. She was heading for the ute. 'So don't worry, the moment we get back to the farm I'll start packing. You'll be rid of me as soon as I can book a flight.' She yanked the passenger door open. Eyes on the ground near the ute's door, her voice hitched to a stop. She snorted a laugh. 'And you can save your stupid rubber snake tricks.'

Rubber snake? What the hell was she talking—*Oh shit!*

'Maya, don't!' Gus moved like he'd been stuck with a cattle prod. In a second, he was beside her, grabbing her arm, stopping her from reaching down to what was definitely not rubber.

Just as he yanked her away from the ute, the snake reared.

Chapter Thirty-Three

Eastern Brown. Maya was no expert on Australian snakes, but the colour of the one disappearing into the bushes was definitely brown. Whereas the colour on Gus's face was … just disappearing.

'Did it bite you?' Gus's concerned expression set off a wave of guilt at the tongue lashing she'd just given him.

'No.' But if he hadn't got to her when he had … She swallowed. 'What about you?' she asked, chest tightening.

Gus shook his head.

Maya slumped against the pick-up. *Thank God.*

Gus scooped up the water bottle he'd dropped and held it out to Maya as he joined her against the car. She took a shaky gulp.

'Thanks,' she said, handing the bottle back to him.

Gus's gaze locked with hers. He gave her a tight-lipped nod before taking his own swig from the bottle—he knew she wasn't just thanking him for the drink of water.

'I'm sorry.' Maya braved a look at Gus. 'I shouldn't have said what I did.'

Face drawn, he stared down the fire trail. The deserted road was the stuff of touristy postcards; a coppery dirt trail, a cloudless blue sky, endless bush. All that was missing was a beaten-up four-wheel drive stirring up dust as it came around the bend.

'I'm the one who should be apologising,' Gus said after a while. 'For before. For losing it. I was talking out my arse, because you had the coward bit right.' He flicked her a quick glance and heaved a sigh. 'I'm petrified, Maya. Scared stiff of losing my brother again and of letting everyone around me down while I go off and do something that might end up being a total failure.'

He caught her gaze with his. 'Thing is, I'm pretty sure you figured out I was scared because you're scared, too. Scared that you're not good enough, scared that taking Michael's place beside your dad might mean letting go of your brother.' He took her hand and squeezed it. 'It's alright to be scared. There are so many unknowns. It'd be weird if we weren't scared of stepping off the path. But I didn't mean what I said before. I don't blame you for Pat's accident. I hate myself for saying that. None of this is your fault, Maya. I don't want you walking away from this thinking you are in any way to blame for Pat's—but especially my—mistakes.'

Maya blinked back the heat in her eyes. They were stuck in the middle of nowhere with no transport, no reception and the very real possibility that Patrick was seriously hurt and Gus might not get to him in time.

The cord around her wrist suddenly felt too tight.

'Hey, look on the bright side—' Gus forced a smile across his features, '—if we get hungry at least it's hot enough to fry eggs on the bonnet waiting for the rescue party.'

Maya couldn't even bring herself to shake her head at his pathetic attempt to lighten the situation.

Eggs? Maya twisted to look behind her. 'We have eggs?'

'Yeah, in the back. I was meant to drop them at a neighbour's.' There was a distinct frown in Gus's voice. 'Why? You hungry?'

'Wait here,' she told Gus and shot around to the back of the pick-up.

'Not like I have any other options.' His terse voice followed her to the back of the car.

She ignored him because, sure enough, there they were, two dozen of them; some white, some brown. All perfect in their shiny smoothness!

She plucked four from their cardboard tray and carefully carried them to the front of the ute. It was a crazy idea. No more than urban legend. It may not even work.

But if it worked for MacGyver, it might just work for her.

Chapter Thirty-Four

She was nuts. Heatstroke, maybe? Gus squinted up into the morning sun. It had the promise of an angry glare but not enough punch yet to have someone acting all bonkers. And yet, here was Maya, cradling a bunch of eggs to her chest as she rounded to the front of the ute with determination.

Eyes half wild with some cooky idea, she flapped at him with her free arm. 'Pop the bonnet for me.'

Shock. That had to be it. Although Gus had never seen shock manifest in this kind of loopy disorientation.

'Gus, hurry up!' Maya patted the bonnet impatiently.

Gus drew in a slow, patient breath. 'I have a better idea. Why don't we get into the ute and have another drink of water? It's getting hot.' He held his half-full water bottle out to her again and shook it, hoping it was enough to entice her to ditch the eggs along with her harebrained idea.

She huffed. 'I'm not delusional or delirious …'

Maybe he was, since she was now reading his thoughts.

'I want to try something that might get us out of here,' she said, tapping the bonnet again.

Gus caught his bottom lip between his teeth. She didn't look like she'd lost her marbles—other than the fact she was cradling a handful of eggs like they were of the oh-so-delicate-Faberge variety rather than the about-to-be-scrambled kind. But, he climbed into the cab of the ute and pulled the bonnet release.

He caught a glimpse of her smile before her face disappeared behind the upturned hood. A moment later, a puff of steam rose into the sky.

He was halfway out of the cab when her sharp 'No!' stopped him.

'I need you in the car,' she said from behind the hood.

What on earth is she doing? He slid back into the driver's seat but craned his body around the windscreen to see that Maya was—

'Cracking eggs into the radiator?' He blinked, rubbed a hand over his eyes, but nope, he wasn't hallucinating. The girl was literary cracking eggs into his ute's radiator. 'How the hell is that meant to get us out of here?'

She glanced over at him without missing a beat. 'Science,' she said and kept right on cracking like she was baking a damn cake. Another egg plopped into the cooling system. A bloody expensive-to-repair cooling system!

Gus wiped a shaky hand down his face. If he wasn't so desperate to get to the hospital, he'd be having palpitations at the damage this was going to wreak on his ute.

'That's right, wipe that faithless look off your face.' Maya sent the last egg down into the radiator. 'The hot coolant is meant to bind the egg and clog the leak. That's what MacGyver tells me.'

'MacGyver?' *Was she for real?* 'You're cracking eggs into my radiator because you saw it on *MacGyver*?'

'Not just MacGyver—' her voice, all snappy and defensive, came from behind the upturned bonnet, '—the Mythbusters also proved it works.'

The only thing all of this proved was that she was certifiable. Heat stroke or shock or whatever, she'd gone round the bend, mistaking a bunch of eggs for her lost marbles. Gus threw his hands in the air and slumped back in his seat. 'MacGyver *and* the Mythbusters? Well, in that case let me give you a few more eggs.'

Her head—minus the all-important marbles—poked around the side of the bonnet. By the raised eyebrow and tight line of her mouth Gus had no doubt she'd picked up on the subtle-as-a-sledgehammer sarcasm in his voice.

'Just turn the engine over, will you?' she said and disappeared behind the bonnet again.

Gus shook his head. Resigned, he turned the key in the ignition. The ute shuddered to a shaky start. Any second, Gus waited for it to cough, splatter and die. Any second now, any second …

Gus scratched his slack jaw; the engine kept on rumbling. And rumbling. And rumbling. Then, came a whoop. Followed by the slap of the bonnet clapping shut.

Gus sat up straighter in his seat as Maya hopped in beside him, eyes wide with barely contained excitement. 'It worked!'

Jaw still hanging slack, Gus blinked. 'For real?'

He didn't doubt her ability when it came to fixing cars, but they were talking MacGyver hacks with eggs, for sheep's sake.

'It might not get us all the way to the hospital, but at least we don't have to trek for hours to have a shot at getting somewhere with mobile reception,' she said. 'What are we waiting for? Let's get out of here.'

Gus threw the ute into reverse, trying hard to quash the ball of hope rolling around in his chest like a hay bale. If this scrambled egg hack managed to get him to his brother, he'd watch every bloody episode of *MacGyver*. Twice.

Chapter Thirty-Five

Maya held on to the passenger-side handle as Gus pushed the pick-up along the uneven dirt road as quickly as the patched-up radiator allowed. Her eyes stayed mostly glued to the hood for signs of burnt egg—when she wasn't sneaking glances at Gus. Jaw locked and fingers gripping the steering wheel knuckle-white, it was like he was convinced the extra pressure would make the car go faster.

Maya pulled her cell out of her pocket and frowned.

'Anything?' Gus asked.

She shook her head.

Gus's knuckles turned translucent.

'He'll be okay.' As soon as the words were out, Maya bit her lip—she couldn't vouch for the truth of them, and Gus knew that.

She returned her attention to the bumpy road ahead. *Please let us get in range of a cell tower soon.*

'You know what scares me almost as much as Pat not being okay?' Gus's quiet voice rolled over her thoughts. 'Living a life walking in a badly fitting pair of shoes.' He met her eyes for a brief moment, then turned to the road again.

'Promise me something,' he said, suddenly whipping back her way, a newfound resolve etched across his face. 'You've got to promise me you'll step into the pair of shoes that's right for you when you get home, no matter how bloody shit scared you are, you've got to do it, Maya. You can't walk around worrying that you'll step on a dead man's toes.'

Maya tore her eyes away from the intensity in Gus's.

Too much. Too raw.

Too close.

He was too close to her biggest fear. And her most desperate want. And the two were clashing inside her chest, fighting each other to get out.

'Maya.' His hand landed heavy and pleading on her arm. 'You're good enough, you hear me? More than good enough. You have this car running on eggs, for sheep's sake!' His grip tightened. 'You've got to do this, promise me.'

She couldn't look at him. She couldn't. If she did he'd see the glint of hope in her eyes and he'd push and push until she gave in and made him a promise she wasn't sure she could keep.

But could she? *None of this is your fault ... You're good enough.* They were Gus's words. But it was Michael's voice whispering them to her now.

She shifted in her seat, eyes finding her cell. 'I should check the reception again.'

The air around Gus stilled. He didn't need to say anything for her to hear his disappointment.

'Two bars!' This time she grabbed Gus's arm. He startled. Thankfully not enough to cause another car-on-tree incident.

'Pull over, quick!' she said.

But Gus had already slowed the pick-up and brought it to a stop at the side of the road.

He had his cell out and up to his ear in seconds.

'Pick up, pick up, pick up,' he whispered. The tendons in his throat pulled rope-tight, then released on a groan. 'Voicemail.'

Quickly, Gus dialled another number. Seconds later, his eyes slid shut. 'Of course, Dad's got his phone turned off.' He looked over at

Maya. 'Think your egg whites can get us all the way to the hospital?'

Maya held her breath as she listened for any sputters in the engine. The smooth hum was encouraging but she didn't want to make any grand promises. 'At least into town,' she hedged. Once there, they'd find a way to get Gus to see Pat.

She'd make sure of it.

Chapter Thirty-Six

Barangaroo Creek base hospital was air-conditioned. That didn't stop Gus breaking out in a sweat the moment he and Maya stepped through the front doors.

He beelined for the reception desk, almost bowling over an elderly guy pushing along an IV stand. The last time Gus had seen a fluid-filled bag dangling from one of those had been four years ago, next to Pat's bed as he lay comatose and intubated fighting for his life.

Gus's stomach clamped at the memory—or rather the possibility that it might be a new reality.

He blinked the image away. 'I'm here to see Pat Robertson,' he said. 'He came off a—' Gus swallowed and opened his mouth to try again but the word just wouldn't come.

'He was in an accident,' Maya finished for him. 'Yesterday afternoon.'

The woman at the counter tapped something into her computer and frowned. 'There's a Mr Robertson in room 64 but I don't think—'

'Thank you!' Gus said, already on the move.

The hospital wasn't big and with each door they passed, the corridor walls seemed to edge closer. By the time they reached room 64 less than a minute later, Gus's hands were shaking. Maya took hold of one and squeezed. He looked down at their joined fingers, then up at her shaky smile. After all the crap he'd put her through, she was still here.

Holding on to the anchor of Maya's hand, Gus forced air into his lungs and stepped into the hospital room.

And found an empty bed.

Beside it, his brother sat in his wheelchair flicking through his phone, not a scratch on him apart from the grooves digging into his forehead as he looked up and frowned across at Maya and him.

'You didn't need to come all the way to the hospital. I thought Mum left you a message.'

Mirroring Pat's expression, Gus ran his eyes over his brother again. No bandage, no hidden IV, no sign of any injury. 'She did. Said there's been an accident.'

'Yeah,' Pat pocketed his mobile and shook his head. 'Dad was keen to go out on the quads. We found an ewe caught in some fencing. Stupid animal knocked him over after he untangled it and the silly old bugger banged his head on the fence post and down he went.'

Gus stepped further into the room. 'Dad was the one hurt?'

Pat nodded. 'Smashed his phone and broke his arm in the process. Lucky I was there is all I can say.'

Gus swallowed. 'He's going to be all right though?'

'He's cranky as a flyblown ram, won't stop bellyaching about the broken arm and how long it'll keep him off the machinery—' Pat rolled his eyes, '—but he'll be fine.'

Gus glanced at the empty bed.

'They've taken him for a couple of tests to make sure he doesn't have concussion,' Pat explained. 'Once he's got the all clear, the old codger can go home. Thank God, too. Mum's gone to get her third coffee for the day and it's not even lunchtime. That's how mental he's been driving us with all his whining.'

Gus's relief left his chest in a quick whoosh. Limbs suddenly heavy, he sank onto the empty bed.

'I thought it was you,' he said, not looking at his brother. 'That you'd come off the quad … That you'd ended up here again and …' He ran a hand, unsteady and clammy once more, down his face. 'I thought the whole nightmare was happening all over.'

'I might go find Jen,' Maya said quietly from the foot of the bed. 'Get us a couple of coffees, too?'

Gus swallowed, but nodded at the question in her voice.

As soon as Maya left, Pat wheeled himself closer. 'Gus, look at me.'

The last thing Gus wanted was to look at his brother, but he forced himself to. He locked on eyes the colour of freshly turned earth, eyes that could have been his own.

'It isn't happening again,' Pat said, brows raised, making their point. 'No-one can guarantee there won't be more accidents, but you've got to stop thinking every little thing will end up in one. You've got to let it go.'

Gus grimaced. 'I've tried.' It wasn't that easy.

'It wasn't your fault,' Pat said.

The sting behind Gus's eyes started immediately, the way it always did when he heard his brother say those words. Pat had never laid any blame for the accident on Gus's head. That somehow made it worse. So Gus piled enough on for the both of them.

He swiped at his watering nose. 'It was. I was the one who nagged and pushed to race and—'

'Gus, it was *not* your fault.'

Gus opened his mouth to argue, but no sound came out. The calm conviction in Pat's voice gave those six short words the weight of six thousand—and set off a fresh sting in Gus's eyes. *Bloody hell.*

Pat leaned forward, squeezed his arm. 'I drove the quad. My hands were steering. I hit the ditch. It was not your fault.'

Pat's hand blurred on Gus's arm. He pulled his arm free and closed his eyes, let his head drop and his fear—salty and wet—slide down his face. He was so tired. Of trying to fix something he couldn't fix, of trying to be someone he didn't want to be.

'I don't want to run the farm.' As soon as he said the words, his heart fought to claw its way out of his chest. He'd never said them out loud, never told Pat or his parents. It was as good as cursing the respected Robertson name. Any second now, he'd be struck by lightning, right through the roof of Barangaroo Creek base hospital. He bunched the stiff hospital waffle blanket in his hands.

'Tell me something I don't know.'

Gus's eyes flew open. 'What do you mean, you know?' He'd been careful never to let on he wanted off the land. How the hell did Pat even know?

'Don't worry, the old man has no idea. You did a good job of pulling the wool over most people's eyes.' Pat glanced at the door to the room, almost as though he expected their father to suddenly appear. The last thing Gus needed right at that moment.

'You always made sure you took an interest in everything to do with the farm,' Pat went on, 'made the right noises when Dad asked questions, but your eyes sort of went vacant, like someone switched a light off and shut a door somewhere inside. Total opposite to what they do when you talk about your computer graphic projects.' Pat raised a knowing eyebrow. 'Also, I might have seen the student workbook for your …' Pat drew air quotes, ' … surfing trip.'

Gus threw his brother a sour look. 'You went snooping in my bag?'

'Didn't need to. You forgot to zip it up. I did it for you.' Another raised eyebrow.

Gus flicked at the edge of the hospital blanket. 'Thanks.' The thought of his father finding the evidence of his deception sent ice down Gus's spine.

'You've got to tell him, mate.'

A shudder galloped down Gus's back. Tell him. Tell their father. Pat wasn't talking about just the Sydney trip. The serious line of his brother's mouth spoke of something bigger than that.

Flick. Flick. Flick. Common sense would be to just rip the Band-

Aid off in one go, but what if that caused more damage? What if it ripped open the safe, predictable, pre-programmed life he'd known for the past eighteen years and left an uglier wound than before? Gus wasn't sure he had the strength to face that kind of painful mess.

There was another, less confronting, option. 'How about I just help him see that you're a better choice for taking over the farm and leave it at that.'

Pat's snort gave Gus a general idea of what his brother thought of that suggestion. He edged his wheelchair as close as he could to the metal frame of the bed and got right up into Gus's face. 'How about you stop dancing around the sheep shit for once in your life and take a stand. The old man might surprise you.'

It was Gus's turn to snort. The only surprise would be if their father allowed him to gather up his stuff before throwing his disappointment of a son off the farm.

Gus went to flick the edge of the blanket again for good measure, but Pat dragged his hand away. 'Look, I appreciate you wanting to help Dad see that I'm capable, but I've realised that's my fight, not yours. It's something I have to do, just like telling him you don't want to take over the farm is something *you* have to do. I can't go around blaming others for not getting what I want if I don't try to fight for it, and neither can you, so quit being a sheeple and tell him the truth. He won't like it, crusty old bugger that he is, but he might eventually come around to accept it.'

'You think?' Despite the heavy sarcasm in his voice, Gus couldn't mask the faint note of hope.

Pat sat back in his wheelchair, the smile on his face just as much dare as it was encouragement. 'Only one way to find out.'

***

That night, Gus found his father at their kitchen table after dinner.

'How's the arm?' Gus's gaze ran the length of his father's elbow-to-wrist cast resting next to a bowl of custard covered apple pie and the *Barangaroo Creek Gazette* on the table in front of him.

'Annoying.' The man glowered at his broken left arm. 'I'm going to need all hands on deck until this thing comes off.'

Gus pulled out a chair and sat. 'Good thing Pat's back on the quad then,' he offered cautiously.

A grunt and a nod. It wasn't much, but it was acknowledgement enough. Gus risked a smile for his brother. Now to take a risk for himself.

'I'll do whatever needs to be done for the rest of the summer, but after that …' He pulled the papers from his back pocket and pushed them across the table.

His father frowned. 'What is this?'

'Application forms for computer animation courses.'

A scoff this time. 'Not this nonsense again.' He pushed the papers back towards Gus. 'There's no time for this. Not while working on the farm and doing your Ag course.'

Gus took a deep breath. 'You're right.' He forced himself to look his father in the eye. 'Which is why I don't want to work the farm or do the Ag course.' Gus's eyes widened. He'd said the words. He'd finally said the words to his father. His shoulders lightened even as his lungs constricted at the man's stony expression.

'You want to turn your back on your family so you can play make believe on your computer?'

Gus's gut clenched. 'No. I want to step aside to do what I love and leave the farm to the person who's always wanted to run it.' He leaned forward, needing the man to understand. 'Don't you see? I've tried. I've really, really tried, but for me it'll never be more than going through the motions, because I've never wanted it, Dad, not like Pat or you. I've never wanted it.'

Something dimmed in his father's eyes like the words had broken the old man's heart.

Gus blinked rapidly at the hurt on his father's face. As much as he didn't see eye to eye with him, it killed him to let the man down.

But it would kill him to continue pretending to be someone he didn't want to be.

Gus slid the application papers back towards his father. 'I know this isn't what you'd hoped, but it's what I really want to do, Dad.'

Something flashed across his father's face. Disappointment or regret, Gus couldn't tell. 'And you'll do it regardless of what I say?'

'I'd prefer to do it with your blessing, but yes.' He'd find a way to do it either way. He had to.

Richard Robertson pulled the bowl of custard covered apple pie closer and speared it with his spoon. 'Then there's nothing more to discuss.'

Gus's chair legs scraped the floorboards, carving a painful gash into the deafening silence. He'd known all along following this path would never secure him his father's approval. Time to make peace with it and move on, no matter how much it cut him up.

He reached for the application papers, but his father shifted his arm, pinning them to the table with his cast.

Confused, Gus's eyes sought the brown ones across the table.

'I'll get them back to you later tonight,' he said and returned his attention to his dessert.

Gus nodded. He didn't dare risk a smile until he'd made it to the living room where Pat and Maya waited for him.

'How did it go?' Pat asked as soon as he'd shut the door.

Gus gave the two of them a sideways look. 'Like you haven't been eavesdropping.'

Pat and Maya exchanged a *busted* glance.

'So he's reading the application forms?' Pat asked.

'Yeah.' Gus still couldn't believe it.

'That's good!' Maya said.

Gus's gaze snagged on her larger-than-life smile. It *was* good. And he had her to thank for so much of it. He sank down beside her on the couch.

'So, MacGyver,' he said, taking her hand in his, 'you think the next five weeks is enough time for you to introduce me to this radiator repair guru of yours?'

Epilogue

'Pass me the anti-squeal grease, will you, Dad?'

Maya's father handed her the bottle of grease paste along with a quick smile. 'I can finish that for you if you like.' He nodded at the exposed wheel hub. 'I know you've got things to prepare for tomorrow.'

'Thanks, Dad, but I'm almost done here.' This was the last brake pad she had to replace, then she was finished for the day.

He was right, she needed to put some final touches on tomorrow's workshop program, but most of it was done. Preparing for it had been surprisingly enjoyable. And way more painless after she finally allowed Gus to put together a series of animations to go with the different parts of the workshop. She was pretty sure hers would be the first auto shop class that had an animated mechanic gorilla showing students how to change a tyre or replace a set of spark plugs.

Speaking to crowds wasn't exactly her thing, so the videos were a great go-to if she stuffed up or froze. Gus might have been convinced she'd take to the whole thing like a sheep to grass, but she still wasn't sure if she was excited or just plain nervous.

She smiled to herself while she installed the carrier bolts. If someone had told her a year ago she'd be talking all things car maintenance to a bunch of high school girls, she'd have snorted in their general direction.

'How many of these auto shop lesson days are they wanting you to do?' her father asked from behind the bunged-up exhaust he was fixing on the next hoist over.

'At this point only two. Mind you, I got emails from another couple of schools interested, so there could be more.'

There weren't a great deal of female motor mechanics, and Maya loved the idea of sharing the possibilities of a motor mechanic career with young girls, even if the prospect made her nervous.

Her father grunted. It wasn't a negative sound. Not exactly a positive one either, though.

Maya straightened and looked at his overall-covered back. 'Is me doing these school workshops a problem, Dad?' She'd just assumed he'd be happy for her to do them, but it did take her away from her work at the garage.

'No, no. It's a good thing for you to do. Gets your name out there.' His voice came from behind the muffler a second before his face appeared. 'It's just …' He grabbed a rag and wiped his hands with jerky motions. 'Well, I … It's not the same when you're not here to keep us all in line, is it, boys?' He glanced over his shoulder, first at wiry old Felton, then at Paul spread out at the front desk.

The mechanics nodded and made noises in agreement with their boss, but both sent her knowing grins as soon as her father had turned back to face her.

Maya made a show of double checking the carrier bolts were on tight enough. That way her father couldn't see her grinning to herself. She'd been his apprentice for almost a year now, and even though at first she'd been terrified of making mistakes, of not doing it as well as she knew her brother would have done, Dad had been nothing but encouraging from the first day. Not once did he make her feel inadequate or incompetent. And now he missed her when she wasn't working with him. The realisation sent ripples of warmth through her chest.

'I promise I won't let it get in the way of my hours here,' she said, her smile sincere and just for him.

Maya heard the office door buzzer go off. They all shared front desk duties. Usually, whoever had their hands free or cleanest would tend to the new customer. Paul had been at the desk just now, so Maya went about getting her last tyre to finish her job.

'What can we do for you?' Paul asked the customer.

'Think I busted my radiator,' came a mumble-like male reply.

Maya's hands stilled on the tyre as her breath did much the same in her lungs—busted radiators would forever have a stop-start effect on her heart.

She missed him far more than she should, considering they spoke at least once a week and messaged far more than that. It wasn't the same as breathing the same air as him, though, or tugging his Akubra lower over his eyes when he made a stupid joke, or sliding her fingers into his warm, callused hand and having him squeeze in that way only Gus somehow could. Although, his hands may not be as callused anymore now that he was sitting in lecture halls and in front of his computer every day.

Shaking all thoughts of Gus aside, Maya heaved the tyre into place.

'Pity I didn't have any eggs in the back seat, otherwise I'd have fixed it myself.'

The lug she'd been tightening slipped in Maya's hand.

She craned around her hoist, eyes zeroing in on the front desk—and dropped the lug altogether.

'Gus!' He was here! Know-it-all grin under his tattered cowboy hat and all.

She covered the workshop floor in lightning speed and launched herself at him. He caught her with a laugh and an *oof* as she nearly sent them both onto the shopfront floor.

His arms squeezed her tighter to him and she drank him in. The solid feel of him, the dust and heat smell of him.

'Hi,' he said after a little while, arms not showing any signs of letting her go anytime soon.

She pulled away enough to look up at him and finally asked,

'What are you doing here?'

'Getting my radiator fixed.'

Maya heard her father chuckle from the workshop floor. Was he in on this? Had he known Gus was coming? She wouldn't put it past the two of them to plot something like this.

She tightened her arms around Gus's waist again. Less in affection and more in warning. 'I don't really care why you're here. What's important is how long you're staying.' It was summer in Sydney right now. That meant he still had a month, maybe more, of his university break left.

Gus pursed his lips like he was thinking about it. She tightened her arms in a quick *spill-all-now* squeeze.

Gus grinned and dropped a kiss on her nose. 'That depends on how long it'll take you to help me tick off the items on my American must-do list. By my calculations, it could take a year or so, since I'll be a bit busy with my digital animation course at Columbia and all that but—'

'You transferred?' Maya asked. 'How?'

He nodded, his grin taking over his face. 'It's just for a year, then there's a review, but if I keep my grades up, I might have the option of finishing my degree here.'

Speechless. His sudden presence and now this news … All Maya could do was stare up at him and gape.

The grin she loved so much wavered and something like uncertainty tugged it off Gus's face. 'Say something.'

She did, in the only way she could when she knew no words would come out right—she tugged Gus's cowboy hat lower over his eyes and pressed her lips to his.

All the while, her mind was floating with all the things and places she wanted to put on Gus's list.

Starting with a spin down the highway in her beloved Big Bird, the little boomerang Gus gave her at the airport dangling from the rearview mirror—on a familiar piece of leather string.

Also by Kat Colmer

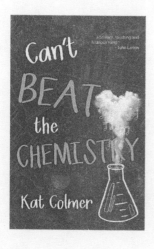

Ionic and covalent bonds are a piece of cake for MJ. But human bonds are a little harder ...

There are only two things MJ wants in her final year of high school:

1) Glowing grades and ...

2) to convince uber-smart, chiselled-jaw Jason they'd be a winning team outside the science lab as well as in.

Tutoring deadbeat drummer, Luke, isn't part of the plan. After all, he has average intelligence, takes disorganised notes and looks like a partied-out zombie at their study sessions! Not even his taut biceps will win MJ over.

But MJ learns that she could be tutored in a few life lessons too: That sometimes there's good reason to skip chemistry tutorials. That intelligence is so much more than a grade average.

And that sometimes you can't beat the chemistry.

About the author

Kat Colmer is a Sydney-based author and teacher librarian who writes coming-of-age stories with humour and heart. Her debut novel *The Third Kiss* was published by Entangled Teen (2017) and her second young adult novel *Can't Beat the Chemistry* was released in 2019.

Kat has a Diploma of Education with a Masters in Teacher Librarianship and loves working with teens. Having spent a significant portion of her childhood in Germany, Kat speaks fluent German and is looking forward to the day she'll be able to read one of her novels in Deutsch. When not writing, teaching or reading the latest in YA fiction, Kat spends time with her two resident YA critics—aka her children.

Remind Me Why I'm Here is her third novel.